W9-AFE-832

Two men appeared out of nowhere.

One of them grabbed Jupiter and dragged him into a waiting car.

The second pointed a pistol at Bob and Pete. "If you value your lives," he said, "don't follow us!"

He jumped into the car and it roared off toward the highway.

Jupiter was gone!

The **Mystery**
of the
Deadly Double

The Three Investigators in

The
Mystery
of the
Deadly Double

By William Arden

Based on characters created by Robert Arthur

Random House New York

Originally published by Random House in 1978.
First Random House paperback edition, 1981.
Revised edition, 1985.

Library of Congress Cataloging in Publication Data:
Arden, William.
    The Three Investigators in The mystery of the deadly double.
    (The Three Investigators mystery series ; 28)
    Originally published as: Alfred Hitchcock and The Three Investigators
in The mystery of the deadly double. 1978.
    SUMMARY: The Three Investigators foil a plot to kidnap the son of a
political leader in an African colony.
    [1. Mystery and detective stories.   2. Kidnapping—Fiction]
I. Arthur, Robert.   II. Title.   III. Title: Mystery of the
deadly double.   IV. Series.
PZ7.A6794Te   1985   [Fic]   83-26940
ISBN: 0-394-86428-X (pbk.)

Manufactured in the United States of America
1 2 3 4 5 6 7 8 9 0

Contents

Introduction by Hector Sebastian

Welcome, mystery fans.

You're about to start an adventure in which The Three Investigators face one of the most amazing coincidences of their careers. An ordinary trip to an amusement park turns into a nightmare that tests all the ingenuity of the young detectives. Danger and confusion are waiting for them behind every corner as they try to solve this mystery.

The boys are confronted by kidnappers, cryptic messages, and an enemy who tracks them to their secret headquarters. They set out to follow the devious trail of a fugitive boy and wind up embroiled in a case of international intrigue. It's almost more than these crack private eyes can handle.

The case demands the deductive powers of all three boys. Jupiter Jones, normally the brains of the firm, is the puzzled target of the crooks, so he's unable to direct the team full time. This thrusts Pete Crenshaw, the most athletic Investigator, into the limelight. Pete has to ignore his uneasiness and take on a more daring role than usual. And Bob Andrews, the meticulous research man of the group, gets a chance to prove he's as smart as he is reliable.

From their hidden house trailer in The Jones Salvage Yard to the Mexican border, the boys follow and are followed.

But I'll leave it up to you to find out who catches whom in the end . . . and what the startling coincidence that turns their lives upside down is!

—HECTOR SEBASTIAN

The
Mystery
of the
Deadly Double

1

False Alarms

"Nobody move!" Pete Crenshaw cried.

Bob Andrews and Jupiter Jones froze. The boys were in their secret headquarters inside an old mobile home, where they ran their junior detective firm, The Three Investigators. The old house trailer was carefully hidden under piles of junk in The Jones Salvage Yard, but there was always the danger that someone would stumble upon one of the secret entrances to it. Bob and Jupe looked carefully around their small office and listened intently. Had Pete heard something threatening?

"What . . . what's wrong, Pete?" Bob whispered.

Pete glared fiercely at his two friends.

"Somebody," he declared, "stole my lunch!"

Bob gaped. "Your . . . your lunch? That's all you—!"

"Your lunch, Second?" Jupiter echoed, incredulous.

The tall Second Investigator laughed. "Just a joke. Besides, my lunch is important. I'm getting hungry."

"A poor joke," Jupiter said sternly. "False alarms are very dangerous. You know the story of the boy who cried wolf. That kind of fun can—"

Jupiter, the brainy leader of The Three Investigators, could become a little stuffy, especially when he gave a speech. Bob or Pete often had to bring him down to earth.

3

"Talking won't get you off the hook," Pete interrupted. "I'll bet you couldn't resist a snack when Bob and I were outside in the workshop. I'll bet you swiped my lunch yourself!"

Jupiter reddened.

"I did not!" he exclaimed hotly. A stout boy, if not exactly fat, the First Investigator hated any suggestion that he ate too much.

"Well," Pete insisted, "someone did."

"Maybe you took it out to the workshop, and forgot it," Bob suggested.

"Wherever it is, it can wait," Jupiter said, recovering his self-assurance. "We haven't decided where to go on our outing tomorrow. It's our last chance to do something exciting before school opens again. Since no one seems to want to hire us for a case right now, and we've been working around the salvage yard all summer, I think we should take a real trip. We've all been to Disneyland a lot, so I say we go to Magic Mountain. I've never been there."

"Me, neither," Pete said. "What's it like?"

"It's one of the biggest and best amusement parks in the world, that's all," Bob said eagerly. "It doesn't have the fantasy stuff of Disneyland, but it's got four roller coasters. One of them loops upside down! There're two water chute rides, and do you get soaked! And there's a special kind of Ferris wheel a mile high, and maybe thirty other great rides—all for the admission price. No ticket books or anything. Once you're inside, you just go on any ride you want."

"It sounds pretty good," Pete said.

"Then that's it," Jupiter decided. "And just for some

extra fun, we'll go in style—in the Rolls-Royce! I've already called Worthington, and the car's available tomorrow."

"Wow," Bob said, laughing, "they'll think we're millionaires! I can't wait to see everyone's face when we drive up."

"If I live that long." Pete groaned. "I'm starving. Come on, where'd you guys hide my lunch?"

"We didn't hide it, Pete," Bob insisted.

"No one touched your lunch, Second," Jupiter said in an exasperated voice. "You probably did take it out to the workshop with you. We might as well find it, or we'll never get our plans settled."

Suiting action to words, Jupiter raised the trap door in the floor of the trailer and squeezed down into Tunnel Two. This was the main entrance to Headquarters, consisting of a length of wide metal pipe running under the trailer and the junk that surrounded it. Pete, tall and athletic, practically had to flatten himself on his stomach to get through the pipe, but he slid easily along behind the Investigators' puffing, overweight leader. Bob, the smallest of the three boys, had no trouble at all crawling swiftly in the rear.

They emerged in Jupiter's outdoor workshop, which was in a front corner of The Jones Salvage Yard. The workshop was protected by a sloping six-foot-wide roof which ran around the inside of the junkyard fence. Mounds of junk around the workshop hid the area from view. In it the boys had their printing press and the larger tools that they used to rebuild junk into useful equipment for their detective work. The workshop area also contained a chair, some old crates, and a workbench.

It was on the workbench that Bob spotted Pete's lunch bag.

"See, you did leave it out here," the Records and Research member of the team declared.

Pete picked up the torn paper bag. "But who ate it?"

"You probably ate it yourself, and forgot you did," Jupiter said in disgust.

"Me?" Pete cried. "Forget I ate a good ham sandwich?"

"I'll bet it was rats," Bob said, examining the bag. It had been ripped raggedly open. "They eat anything."

"You think Aunt Mathilda lets rats run loose around the salvage yard? No way!" Pete exclaimed.

"She tries, but not even Aunt Mathilda can keep all the rats out of a big junkyard," Jupiter said, laughing. Jupe's aunt Mathilda was a formidable woman who ran the salvage yard with an iron hand. Her husband, Titus, spent most of his time scouting for new junk to add to the yard. Jupe, who had been orphaned at an early age, had lived with them ever since he could remember.

"Come on, let's see if Aunt Mathilda will give us all some lunch," said Jupe, and he led the way toward the junkyard office. But as he neared the main gate of the yard, he suddenly slowed. "Fellows, have you ever seen that car before?"

Bob and Pete looked toward the entrance. A green Mercedes sedan was parked almost directly across the street from the open gates. No one got out of it.

"It was moving when I first noticed it," Jupiter said slowly. "Just creeping along, and then it stopped."

"So what, Jupe?" Pete said. "Can't a car park around here? Maybe it's a customer for the yard."

"Perhaps," Jupiter admitted, "but no one has gotten out, and I think I saw that same car driving past the entrance earlier this morning. Going just as slowly."

"Hey," Bob exclaimed, "I think maybe I saw it, too! On the street outside the back fence when I was riding over here. Maybe an hour ago."

"Maybe *they* stole my lunch!" Pete said.

"Sure, international lunch thieves!" Bob said dryly.

"Forget your lunch," Jupiter snapped impatiently. He was still watching the motionless car through the open gates. "If you didn't eat it, Bob's right—rats got it. I think I'd like to try to find out what that car's up to."

Bob grinned. "Maybe they're just waiting for a chance to steal another ham sandwich."

"It looks to me as if they're waiting for *something*, Records," Jupiter said. "Let's go and see."

Jupiter had a way of seeing a mystery in almost everything, and an uncanny ability to be right! Bob and Pete had long ago given up questioning even Jupe's wildest hunches. He was wrong sometimes, but not very often.

"Pete, you double back in the yard and sneak up inside the main entrance," Jupiter instructed. "Hide and watch the car from there. Bob and I can go out Red Gate Rover in the back and circle around outside the fence. Bob, you go to the left, and I'll go to the right. We'll observe the car from all sides."

Pete nodded, and watched his partners slip out of the yard through their secret entrance in the back fence. Then he skirted behind some mounds of junk and crept along the inside of the fence to the main gate. He peered around. The Mercedes was still there. Two people seemed to be in it. Pete ducked back hurriedly.

Out of sight, he got down on his stomach and crawled back to the open entrance. Flat on the ground, he peered around again.

"Hello! Lost something? Perhaps I can help?"

Pete gulped. A stocky, sunburned man in a lightweight suit stood directly above him in the entrance. The man had curly brown hair and small blue eyes, and was smiling politely. He seemed amused at the sight of Pete crawling flat on his stomach in the yard.

"I–I—" Pete stammered, feeling foolish, "I lost my ball. I was looking . . . for . . . it."

"No ball came out this way," the man said solemnly.

"I guess it bounced somewhere else," Pete said lamely, and got up.

"Bad luck," the sunburned man said, and held out a local road map. "Perhaps you can help me. We seem to be lost."

Pete suddenly saw that the door of the green Mercedes was open, and only one person was still in the car. The stocky man nodded back toward the Mercedes.

"I'm afraid we've been driving in circles, eh? Rather a bad show. Actually, we've been attempting to locate the old mission you chaps have here."

Pete realized that the man had an accent. English, and yet not exactly like any English accent he'd ever heard. The car just held some lost tourists! So much for Jupiter and his hunches!

"Oh, sure." Pete took the map and showed the man where he was, and where the Spanish mission was up the Coast Highway. "It's not so easy to find."

"Quite." The man nodded. "Well, thank you so much."

The man went back to the green Mercedes and the car

drove off. Bob and Jupiter came running up to Pete. Jupiter was staring after the disappearing Mercedes.

"Just tourists, First," Pete said disgustedly, and told them all that had happened. "The guy had a real funny English accent."

"Lost?" Jupiter said, sounding dejected. "That's all?"

"What else, First? We're not even on a case," Pete said.

Jupiter was glum but thoughtful. "It's a possible story since they were foreigners, but—"

"Jupe!" Pete groaned. "They were lost! That's all!"

"And we've got more planning to do for our trip!" Bob said.

"Sure," Pete said. "After we eat some lunch."

Bob and Jupiter looked at each other. There was a bin of old tennis balls near the main gate. Bob and Jupe grabbed balls and began to hurl them at Pete, who ran off into the yard laughing.

2

Kidnapped!

Up early the next morning, Bob dressed quickly and hurried down to the kitchen. As he raced through his breakfast, his father put down his newspaper and watched him with a smile.

"An important investigation this morning?" Mr. Andrews said.

"Not today, Dad. We're going to Magic Mountain—in the gold-plated Rolls-Royce. With Worthington driving us!"

Mr. Andrews whistled admiringly. "Three elegant young fellows, eh? I'm afraid that growing up is going to be a little dull for you."

"Not if Jupe grows up with us!"

"No," Mr. Andrews said, laughing, "I guess not."

"We'll probably be kind of late, Dad, but we'll try to be home by dinnertime," Bob called as he ran out the door.

He rode his bike through the bright morning streets of Rocky Beach to the salvage yard and turned in at the main gate. Pete was sitting on the stoop of the yard's office cabin, looking at a magnificent sight. A Rolls-Royce of somewhat advanced age, with huge headlights and a hood as long and black and shining as a grand piano, stood in the salvage yard. Luxurious as the great car would have been in just simple, lustrous black, it outdid itself with one more touch—all the trimming, even the bumpers, was plated in dazzling gold!

"Wow!" Bob said in awe. "I always forget what a beauty it is until we see it again."

A tall, lean man in a chauffeur's uniform stood beside the car, gently rubbing some of the gold-plated trim with a soft cloth. His long, good-humored face smiled at Bob.

"Even I do, Master Andrews, when I must sometimes drive a different machine," the chauffeur, Worthington, said.

Jupiter had first won the use of the fantastic old car in a contest, and later a grateful client had arranged for the boys to use the car anytime they wanted to. Since no one but Worthington ever drove the car for the rental agency that owned it, he had become a good friend of the Investigators'. He still insisted on treating the boys exactly as he would the oldest and wealthiest tycoon. But now his eyes twinkled.

"An important case this time, Master Andrews?" he said.

"Not this time, Worthington," Bob explained. "We're just going on a trip to Magic Mountain, and thought it would be fun to go in the Rolls."

"An outing? Splendid!" Worthington declared. "Who deserves a holiday more than The Three Investigators? I shall report our destination to the company, and fuel the machine while we wait for Master Jones."

The tall chauffeur got into the Rolls-Royce and drove out of the salvage yard. Bob turned quickly to Pete.

"Speaking of Jupe, where is he?"

"In Headquarters, making some plans," Pete said. "He wouldn't tell me about what."

"Come on, let's find out."

They crawled through Tunnel Two and emerged through the trap door into the hidden trailer. Jupiter was hard at work at the desk, colored brochures spread around him.

"Worthington's here, Jupe," Bob said hopefully. "Ready?"

"In a few moments, Records." The stout leader of the trio continued working for a minute, then sat back looking quite pleased with himself. "There, I think that does it."

"Does what?" Pete asked uneasily.

"Completely plans our excursion!" Jupiter declared, beaming. "I have taken a map of Magic Mountain and laid out the optimum route for covering the most rides in the least time. I have allowed for repeat rides on attractions we might find especially pleasing, plus various alternatives in case of long lines at any given ride or possible shutdowns due to wind conditions or mechanical trouble. Then I have—"

Pete groaned. "Er, Jupe, why don't we just start off to the right or left of the entrance, and hit whatever we come to? I mean, sort of wing it?"

"Just, er, follow our noses?" Bob added.

"Wing it?" Jupiter frowned. "A highly inefficient—"

"Maybe just have fun?" Pete suggested.

"Well," Jupiter said stuffily, "if you don't want my plan, I suppose you don't have to accept it."

Miffed, Jupiter looked lovingly at his plans, then

shrugged and dropped them into the wastebasket. Pete and Bob cheered. Jupiter finally had to grin. The three boys hurried down through the trap door and out into the yard.

Worthington and the Rolls-Royce were back. Laughing excitedly, the boys piled into the magnificent car as Worthington held the door open.

"To Magic Mountain, my good man!" Jupiter intoned.

"Yes, sir." Worthington smiled. "Very good, sir."

Magic Mountain was some distance to the east of Rocky Beach, inland through southern California's coastal mountains. Worthington drove the great old car out of town on the back county highway. They had reached the first slopes of the dry, dusty foothills when Worthington suddenly spoke.

"Gentlemen, you stated, I believe, that you were involved in no investigation at present?"

"Unfortunately, no," Jupiter admitted. "Why do you—?"

"Because, unless I am mistaken, we are being followed!"

"Followed!" all three boys cried at once, turning to look behind.

"Where, Worthington?" Bob said. "I don't see any car."

"It is out of sight around the last curve at present," Worthington said, "but I noticed it the moment we left the salvage yard, and it has been behind us ever since. A green Mercedes sedan."

"A green Mercedes!" Jupiter exclaimed. "You're sure?"

"Automobiles are my profession, Master Jones," Worthington said firmly. "There it is now! And coming closer."

The three junior detectives stared out the back window. There was no mistake. The green Mercedes was directly behind them and was coming rapidly closer!

"It's the same car, all right!" Pete cried.

"So," Jupiter said triumphantly, "they weren't just lost tourists! I was right!"

"I–I guess so," Pete admitted nervously. "Who could they be? What do they want?"

"I don't know, Second," Jupiter said grimly, "and I don't think we want to find out right now."

"Maybe we're going to!" Bob cried in alarm. "They're moving in, Jupe! Gaining on us!"

"Worthington!" Jupiter exclaimed. "Can you lose them?"

"I shall endeavor to do so," Worthington said quietly.

The gold-plated Rolls surged forward as Worthington pressed the accelerator to the floor. They were in the mountains now, and the narrow two-lane highway snaked above steep drops into rocky canyons. Worthington gripped the large steering wheel of the car, hurling the gleaming machine in sharp turns at the edges of the precipices.

The green Mercedes leaped in pursuit. The two cars swerved and squealed around the curves, their wheels perilously close to the gaping chasms below. On a straight road the powerful old Rolls-Royce might have drawn away, but it couldn't match the agility of the smaller, newer Mercedes. Inexorably, the green car came closer.

"They're gaining on us," Pete cried in dismay.

Worthington's voice was calm. "It is too dangerous to try to go any faster in the mountains." He coolly scanned the road ahead. "But perhaps—?"

Worthington leaned forward, staring ahead. The Rolls had just come around a sharp curve and the Mercedes was momentarily out of sight. Worthington suddenly slammed on the brakes, skidded the big car almost to the edge of a sheer drop on the right, and swung back across the highway into a narrow dirt road that led off to the left. Speeding up again, the expert chauffeur drove the gleaming machine down the dusty side road and into the dense growth of live oaks and chaparral.

Behind them the Mercedes roared on past the side road.

"You've lost them!" Bob and Pete cried.

"For the moment," Worthington said. "But they will soon realize we have left the highway. We must drive on swiftly."

He pushed down the accelerator, raced the massive car along the narrow dirt road—and screeched to a jolting stop.

"I'm sorry, boys," Worthington said in dismay.

The dirt road ended in an empty box canyon!

"Drive back to the highway!" Jupiter ordered. "Quickly. Maybe they haven't missed us yet!"

Worthington turned the big car, and drove back toward the main road.

The Mercedes almost hit them head on as they rounded a sharp curve! Worthington swerved half off the road. Before he could recover and turn, two men jumped from the Mercedes and ran up to the Rolls-Royce. They held pistols!

"Out! Now!" one barked. He was a stranger but Pete recognized the second man as the one who had asked him for directions the day before.

Warily, the boys and Worthington got out of the Rolls.

"Now see here, my good man," Worthington protested. "We don't know what—"

"Quiet!" the first man snapped.

The second grabbed a startled Jupiter, tied a gag in his mouth, dropped a heavy bag over his head, and dragged him to the Mercedes! The first man waved his pistol menacingly at Bob, Pete, and Worthington.

"Don't follow us! Not if you value your lives, or want to see him again."

The man turned and ran to the Mercedes. It vanished toward the highway.

Jupiter was gone.

3

A Deadly Mistake

Pete whirled toward the Rolls-Royce.

"We've got to follow them!"

"No, Pete!" Worthington and Bob both cried.

Pete stared. "But we have to try to help Jupe!"

"We will," Worthington said, putting his hand on Pete's shoulder, "but we must not follow them. In a kidnapping you must do exactly what the kidnappers say, then call the police immediately."

"Following them could be dangerous for Jupe," Bob explained. "But we can try to see which direction they're going, and tell the police! The kidnappers don't know we have a phone in the Rolls, so they won't think we can alert the police right away. Hurry, we'll climb that hill while Worthington calls Chief Reynolds!"

While Worthington ran to the car to telephone the police chief of Rocky Beach, Bob and Pete scrambled up the steep slope of a nearby hill. Panting, they reached a high ledge in seconds, and looked toward where the dirt road met the highway.

"I see them!" Bob exclaimed.

"Going south toward Rocky Beach!" Pete said. "And driving pretty slowly!"

"They don't want to attract any attention."

"If Chief Reynolds moves fast," Pete cried, "he could get in front of them! Come on!"

They slid and stumbled down the slope to the Rolls-Royce. Worthington was just giving the license number of the Mercedes, and a quick description of the two men.

"Tell the chief they're driving south on the pass highway toward Rocky Beach," Pete said. "He might be able to block them before they can turn off anywhere."

Worthington repeated Pete's message, and then listened.

"Very good, Chief. We'll remain here until you come."

He hung up, and looked at the boys. "What could they want with Jupiter? You're sure you have no idea who they are?"

"We never saw them before yesterday," Bob said.

"We don't know anything!" Pete wailed.

The three of them looked at each other hopelessly.

Gagged in the darkness under the heavy bag, Jupiter was scared. The Mercedes seemed to be driving slowly, going downhill on what Jupiter guessed was the county highway. Going toward Rocky Beach. What did these men want with him? Who were they? Where were they from with their odd English accents?

He squirmed under the bag in the back seat of the car, and a pistol poked hard in his ribs. One of the men was sitting close beside him.

"Sit still," the man said.

Jupiter tried to speak, to protest, but with the gag tight in his mouth all he could do was gurgle and grunt. "Ummmmffff . . . grrruummmm . . ."

"Keep quiet! Quiet and still, eh? Like a nice, noble little do-gooder."

The unseen man laughed beside him, and the nasty laugh was echoed from the front seat where the other man drove.

But Jupiter tried to talk again, to ask what they wanted with him. Uncle Titus and Aunt Mathilda didn't have any money! Not real money! His grunts and muffled gurglings made him feel like a fish flopping on a beach.

"I said keep quiet! You wouldn't want your father to lose his only son, now would you?"

Under the bag, Jupiter froze. His father? But he had no father! His father had died when Jupe was quite small. Desperately he tried to explain that to his captors.

"Ummmmffff ... ggmmmmmrrrrrr ... nnnuuuhhhh ..."

The pistol poked harder into his ribs.

"I won't tell you again, boy!"

"Ummmmffff ... mmmmmdddd ... mmmmsssssttttt ..."

The man beside him laughed again. "He's a regular stubborn case just like his dad, isn't he, Fred? High and mighty, too, I shouldn't be surprised."

"Maybe we better quiet him down, Walt," the other man said from the front seat.

"Only if we must. I don't much take to carting around a sleeping fat one like him."

"Might be best, though. It's a long trip home. We want him all nice and neat when we brace the big man."

The man beside Jupiter laughed once more. "I can hardly wait to see Sir Roger's face when we tell him we've got young Ian and he better change his tune fast."

Under the bag, Jupiter slowly sat back in the car seat. Sir Roger? Ian? Suddenly he realized what had happened—these men thought he was someone else! Someone whose father was an important man! It wasn't a kidnapping for money—it was some kind of blackmail. To make this Sir Roger, whoever he was, do something these men wanted him to do. But they had made a mistake. They had kidnapped the wrong boy! He tried to tell them.

"Ummmmfffff . . . ! Mssssttttttkkkk . . . nnnnnoooo . . ."

This time the man beside him didn't poke the pistol or tell him to be quiet. The Mercedes seemed to speed up as it reached level ground below the mountains. It turned sharply, wheels squealing, and the force of the turn pushed Jupiter against the corner of the seat. Then he heard the sirens! Police cars! The wailing grew louder. Under the bag Jupiter held his breath. They would save him! . . . The sirens began to fade away behind, and were gone.

"That was a near thing!" the man beside him exclaimed.

"You think they were after us?" the driver said.

"Had to be. They were heading for the mountains. How the devil did they learn about us so fast?"

Jupiter knew at once—the telephone in the Rolls-Royce. His friends had alerted the police immediately. But the kidnappers had escaped. How would the police find him now? He had to tell the kidnappers that they had made a terrible mistake!

"Something went wrong, Walt," the driver said grimly. "Nothing else better go wrong. I won't be caught."

Under the dark bag Jupiter felt suddenly cold. Something else had *already* gone wrong! The men had taken the wrong boy, but they didn't know that yet. Jupe couldn't tell them with the gag in his mouth. And did he want them to know their mistake after all? What would they do if they knew?

They wanted some boy named Ian as a weapon against

his father, so Ian would be safe with them. But would Jupiter Jones be safe?

A police car and a sheriff's car roared down the dirt road and skidded to a stop in a cloud of dust. Chief Reynolds and the county sheriff ran up to Worthington and the boys beside the gleaming Rolls-Royce.

"Did you see them?" Bob cried.

"Did you stop them?" Pete added.

Chief Reynolds shook his head. "We blocked the highway at the first crossroad, and then came straight on here. But we didn't pass them, and they didn't come to the roadblock."

"They must have slipped through before we set up the block," the sheriff said. "Turned off on some crossroad. But they can't have gone far yet, and we've got every available man and car out searching for them."

"This area is in the county, boys, so it's the sheriff's jurisdiction," Chief Reynolds explained, "but in a case like this we all work together. We've already alerted the Los Angeles Police Department also."

"Now," the sheriff said, "we'll search for clues here."

Bob was glum. "I don't think you'll find anything, sir. The kidnappers weren't here long enough to leave any clues."

Bob was right. The police and deputies searched every inch of the dirt road in the vicinity of the kidnapping. They found nothing.

"All right, we'll go back to headquarters," Chief Reynolds decided. "It's time we informed the FBI too."

"At least," the sheriff said, "we have one big advantage this time, thanks to you folks and that Rolls-Royce. We're right on top of the kidnappers, and everyone is searching already."

"Yes, sir," Bob said, dejected, "but searching isn't finding. One car isn't so easy to spot, is it?"

"No, but we've got the whole county covered, and all the roads out blocked. There's no way they can get out of the county!"

Bob and Pete climbed into the Rolls-Royce. Neither of them spoke as Worthington followed Chief Reynolds' car toward Rocky Beach, but they looked at each other uneasily, and knew that they were both thinking the same thing.

The kidnappers must have had some plan in case of roadblocks. Some way to escape, and take Jupiter with them.

4

On the Trail of the Villains

The Mercedes stopped.

Jupiter, in the dark under the heavy bag, had tried to follow the progress of the car, but it had made too many twists and turns. Now he listened for any familiar sounds that might tell him where he was. But there was only an empty silence. No movement anywhere, no sounds of traffic, or people, or the sea.

"Get him out," the driver growled from the front seat.

Jupiter heard the car door open, and hands pushed him out onto his feet. He felt hard ground, and leaves, and grass under his shoes.

"Take the bag off so he can see to walk."

The bag was pulled roughly from over his chest and head. The glare of light through thick trees almost blinded him. He opened and closed his eyes to adjust to the light while the gag was removed from his mouth. It was untied by the stocky man with the curly hair who had first talked to Pete at the salvage yard—the man named Walt who had sat beside him in the car and poked him with a pistol.

"Now be good, eh?" Walt said. "Nice and quiet." He waved his pistol to show he meant business.

Jupiter nodded, but said nothing. Ever since he had

realized that he could be in far more danger if the kidnappers discovered their mistake, he had hoped they wouldn't remove the gag. The boy they thought they had was from their country, whatever it was, and would probably have the same odd English accent. If Jupe spoke, they would know at once that he was the wrong boy—unless he tried to mimic their accent. Jupe thought he could, but it was risky. The slightest mistake could give him away.

The stocky kidnapper watched him for a moment, then turned to the driver.

"Get the bags, Fred."

Jupiter breathed a little more easily. He was safe for the moment. He glanced quickly around. They were at the side of another dirt road, deep among live oaks and thick chaparral, close to the mountains. Nothing was familiar or unfamiliar. They could be anywhere in the back country within a hundred miles of Rocky Beach!

"All right, boy, move," the driver said. "That way."

He was a taller and thinner man than Walt, with dark hair and small eyes sunk deep in weather creases, but he had the same deep sunburn. Apparently both men came from a country where the sun was fierce and constant.

They walked on the grass alongside the road for no more than fifty yards, and turned straight toward the mountains. Jupiter could see no path—only the dense, almost impenetrable brush.

"You go first, Fred, set the pace," Walt said. "You've got the bags."

The driver nodded, set the bags down, and pulled aside a thick bush to reveal the entry to a narrow trail. He pushed the two bags through and vanished into the chaparral.

"You next, boy," Walt ordered.

Jupiter searched for the right bush, pulled it aside, and started through. The tough chaparral suddenly slipped out of his grasp. He threw up his hands to protect his face from the thorny branches, jumped back, and flopped sprawling outside the entrance to the hidden trail. Walt grabbed him and hauled him up, pushing him ahead through the chaparral with a curse.

"Watch that, boy, I might get nervous!"

Jupiter gulped, and hurried along the narrow trail. Walt was close behind with his pistol. The tangled brush closed again, leaving no sign of the hidden path.

Hurrying after the driver, Jupiter failed to see a treacherous root, caught his foot, and sprawled on the ground. He lay panting for a moment, but managed to scramble up before Walt reached him.

The two kidnappers walked rapidly through the dense brush as if they had been there before and knew just where they were going. Jupiter tried to keep pace on the barely visible path, but stumbled and fell twice more before he was pushed out into a narrow box canyon deep in the shadow of the mountains.

A small stone cabin stood close under the towering cliff walls of the canyon. The kidnappers unlocked the cabin door, shoved Jupiter inside, and closed the door.

Alone in the cabin, Jupiter heard the door lock behind him.

At police headquarters, Bob, Pete, Uncle Titus, and Aunt Mathilda sat on a bench against the wall.

"If only we'd taken our emergency signals," Pete moaned.

"They're being repaired, remember?" Bob said. "But

Jupe will think of some way to get in touch with us, Second."

Aunt Mathilda glared at the sheriff and Chief Reynolds.

"Are we going to sit around here all day?" she demanded. "Those kidnappers aren't going to just walk in and give up!"

Chief Reynolds shook his head. "We have every area of the town and county covered, Mrs. Jones, and chasing shadows won't help. In a kidnapping all efforts must be coordinated."

"Every police department in California, Nevada, Oregon, and Arizona has been alerted," the sheriff added. "The FBI has been contacted, and so have the Mexican authorities. The license number of the Mercedes is on the teletype to all the police, and to the Department of Motor Vehicles."

"A team of laboratory experts has gone back to the scene of the abduction to search again," Chief Reynolds said. "We can't do more until we have a lead."

"Then there's nothing to stop you from going out and doing some work yourselves!" Aunt Mathilda declared.

"There's a better chance of catching them quickly," the sheriff said, "by having a central control ready to direct the search the moment a lead is discovered."

Aunt Mathilda was obviously unconvinced, and she glared at the sheriff and Chief Reynolds as they left the room. Her temper wasn't improved by the return of the laboratory team with no results. There were still no clues to the whereabouts of the kidnappers and Jupiter.

"What on earth do they want with Jupiter?" Aunt Mathilda fumed. "Are you boys sure you aren't involved in one of your ridiculous investigations? Poking in other people's business?"

"No, ma'am," Bob declared. "We were just going on an outing to Magic Mountain."

Uncle Titus said, "Neither of you two can think of any reason for this?"

"I wish we could," Pete said.

"If I could just get my hands on those criminals!" Aunt Mathilda raged.

In spite of themselves, Bob and Pete couldn't help smiling at each other. They would hate to be the kidnappers if Aunt Mathilda got to them! Then their smiles faded—it didn't look as if anyone was going to get to the kidnappers!

"If we just had somewhere to start from," Bob said. "I know Jupe would find a way to lead us to him."

"If he can," Pete said. "Those kidnappers seem pretty smart, Records."

Chief Reynolds stood over them. "We'll find out soon how smart they are," he announced. "The sheriff's helicopter men have spotted the Mercedes parked back on old Rattlesnake Road, not three miles from town!"

"Let's go!" the sheriff cried as he appeared from a back room. "We've got them!"

At first, alone in the mountain cabin, Jupiter listened for some time at the locked door. He tried to hear what the kidnappers were saying outside, and wondered how long it would be before they discovered their mistake.

He could hear their voices clearly but could make out only scattered words. They seemed to be talking about plans for a trip, and about someone who wasn't there.

Jupiter suddenly realized that they were waiting for someone. For someone to come, and for something to happen.

But who and what out here in a remote canyon?

He strained to hear better, but it was no use. His stomach sank. What if the person they were waiting for knew the real Ian better than they did? Jupe had to find some way to escape from the cabin, and from the kidnappers!

He looked around the tiny cabin. It was a single bare room without any furniture at all. There were no closets, and only the one door, locked from the outside. The single narrow window was barred, as if the cabin had once been used to store something valuable or dangerous. Perhaps it had held dynamite for rock quarrying, or expensive oil-prospecting tools.

But there was nothing stored in the cabin now, and nothing Jupe could use to escape.

He walked slowly around the stone walls, looking for any weak points. There were none. The walls were at least a foot thick and in good repair. Jupe had nothing to break through the walls with, and that would have made too much noise anyway. There was no way out through the walls, so he turned to the floor.

It was made of wide, rough boards at least an inch thick. They were solid boards with no cracks between them, but they were springy. They bent when Jupiter put his weight on them. He realized that the boards were not on the ground, but were laid across supports. There was a space under the cabin!

On his hands and knees, Jupiter crawled over the whole floor. He found a loose board at the rear, close to the wall! By putting a foot heavily on one end of the short board, he was able to raise the other end far enough to get his hands under it and pull it loose. For once he was glad he was a little overweight!

He raised the board all the way, and saw open space underneath. Silently managing to free one more board, he squeezed down through the opening and began to crawl around the low space on his belly. The ground sloped upward on one side, and he could move under only half the cabin. It was enough. The cabin was built on a raised stone foundation with a few ventilation openings much too small for anyone to crawl through. There was no way out.

Jupiter slowly climbed back up into the cabin.

There was no way out at all.

The police cars parked a short distance below the Mercedes on Rattlesnake Road. The police searched every inch of the silent car.

"Nothing," Chief Reynolds said unhappily. "Not a hint to where they've gone from here."

"People can't just disappear," Aunt Mathilda insisted.

Bob, Pete, and Uncle Titus searched all around the abandoned car. It had been pulled onto a grassy verge at the side of the road.

"Nothing looks like a sign from Jupiter," Bob said glumly.

"There isn't even a footprint," Uncle Titus said.

"They've simply vanished," Chief Reynolds said, staring all around at the thick brush and looming mountains. "They could have taken Jupiter anywhere."

"No," Pete declared suddenly. "I don't think so, Chief. I don't think they could have gone far!"

5

Escape!

"How can you know that, young man?" the sheriff demanded.

"You've found a clue, Pete?" Chief Reynolds exclaimed.

Pete stood near the Mercedes, staring down at the dirt road. He crouched and touched the dirt lightly with his hand.

"Look, sir!" the tall Second Investigator said, and pointed to the ground in front of him. "There's a big patch of soft sand across the whole road here. You can see the tire marks of the Mercedes clearly, but there are no other recent tire tracks or footprints! No other car has come this way today, so they couldn't have left in a car. And they didn't walk away on the road, as far as I can see."

The sheriff nodded as he examined the road around the Mercedes. "The road is pretty dry and dusty everywhere, and there're no footprints."

"You mean," Bob exclaimed, "that they must still be somewhere around here?"

"Yes, Records," Pete said, sounding almost like Jupiter himself. "It's my guess they never crossed the road at all, but went off through the chaparral toward the mountains!"

"Hold on," said Chief Reynolds. "There's grass along this side of the road. They might have walked away on that."

"Possibly," said the sheriff. He turned to two of his deputies. "You, Billings and Rodriguez, walk along the grass in each direction and see how far it goes, and if any footprints emerge onto the road. The rest of us will spread out and look for signs of entry into the brush. Everyone step carefully!"

"And look for anything that looks like a question mark," Bob added. "Or a pile of stones, or a branch broken in a funny way! Jupe and Pete and I leave signs like that for each other when we have to split up on a case."

The police and deputies spread out and moved slowly up and down the road on the side nearest the mountains. The two deputies who were checking the extent of the grass soon reported that it didn't go far, and that there were no footprints on the road where it ended. One searcher found a pile of small stones that could have been a sign from Jupiter. But when the sheriff examined the stones, he saw there was dried mud holding them together. They had obviously been there for some time. Another policeman found a broken branch that seemed to point into the dense brush. But a search of the immediate area revealed no break in the chaparral, and no path.

"Chief?" a policeman called. "Is that anything?"

He pointed to something small and white, low in a bush. It seemed to be a piece of litter. Bob and Pete ran up.

"It looks like—" Bob began.

"One of our cards!" Pete finished. He reached in and took it out. "It is one of our cards! Jupe must have slipped it into the bush when the kidnappers weren't looking!"

"Pull back that brush!" the sheriff ordered.

The deputies and policemen pulled and tore at the chaparral, and quickly discovered the hidden trail.

"It's a path all right," Chief Reynolds declared. "And someone's been along it very recently. Look where the small brush has been broken and flattened!"

Everyone hurried along the narrow trail.

"There!" Bob cried. He pointed to some chaparral that was torn up, as if someone had stumbled and fallen. Nearby, on a small rock, was a tiny white question mark!

"It's Jupe's sign! He was carrying his chalk!" Pete exclaimed.

"Hurry!" Uncle Titus urged. "He must be somewhere ahead, closer to the moun—"

Uncle Titus stopped with his mouth still open. He was listening to something. Then everyone else heard it. A noise like a powerful motor grew louder and louder until it seemed to be right on top of them. Aunt Mathilda pointed to the sky.

"It's a helicopter!"

"Is it one of ours?" the sheriff shouted above the roaring noise of the aircraft as it passed less than a hundred yards above them and swept on toward the mountains.

"No," Chief Reynolds shouted back. "It must be theirs! That's how they intend to escape, Sheriff! It's going to pick up the kidnappers and Jupiter!"

They all stared up at the helicopter until it vanished behind the dense growth of trees above them, its noise slowly fading away into the distance ahead.

"And you said there was no way they could get out of the county, Sheriff!" Aunt Mathilda cried furiously.

"Keep going," the sheriff said grimly. "They must be somewhere ahead on this trail."

"If we can get there in time," Pete moaned. "Before that chopper picks them up."

In the box canyon, the two kidnappers watched the helicopter land in a swirl of dust. The rush of air from the whirling blades whipped their hair and clothing. With the rotors idling, the pilot jumped out of the clear plexiglass bubble. Muffled in a flying suit, helmet, and goggles, the pilot ran to the kidnappers.

"Right on time," the stocky one, Walt, said.

"We've got him!" Fred added, grinning.

The pilot didn't grin in reply. "There're police cars all over the road back there where you left the Mercedes! I think I saw police already coming through the brush!"

"On the path?" Walt scowled. "How did they find it so fast?"

"The kid!" Fred cried. "Those times he fell! I'll bet he left them a trail!"

Walt laughed. "Never mind, eh? It'll take them at least half an hour to get here from the road. By then we'll be up with the birds."

"Don't play games, Walter," the pilot snapped. "Get the boy now. This is too important to our country to make any mistakes."

"Okay," Walt agreed, "let's get him."

"Where is he?"

"In that cabin, locked up tight."

"Good," the pilot said, "but make it fast now."

The three of them trotted across the hard floor of the canyon. Walt unlocked the cabin door.

"All right, boy, rise and shine," he called.

"Walt!" Fred cried. "He's not in here!"

The dim room of the cabin was empty!

"You've let him escape!" the pilot raged.

"Impossible," Walt said. "There's no way out."

They all stared around the deserted cabin.

"Maybe not," Fred said savagely, "but there's no place to hide in here, either, and he's not here!"

"He's gotten out somehow!" the pilot cried.

"All right, don't panic," Walt ordered. "He may have gotten out of the cabin, but he's still in the canyon. That one path is the only way out, and we've had it in full view the whole time. He couldn't have gotten past us, Fred, so he's still somewhere in the canyon behind the cabin. Let's get him!"

The three kidnappers hurried out into the barren canyon, and spread out.

Panting, the boys, the police, and Jupiter's aunt and uncle emerged from the path into the long, narrow canyon. It was more than twenty minutes since the helicopter had passed overhead, and they scanned the canyon apprehensively.

"It's here!" Bob exclaimed.

The helicopter stood far up the canyon with its rotors idling, but even as they watched, the pilot jumped inside and the aircraft began to put on full power for takeoff!

"But it won't be for long!" Pete cried. "Run!"

As they began to run toward the roaring machine, two men appeared from behind a small stone cabin. They each carried a suitcase, and raced to the helicopter.

"They're too far ahead of us!" Chief Reynolds cried.

"You! Stop! Police!" the sheriff shouted as he ran.

But the kidnappers had reached the helicopter. They scrambled into the bubble, and as the search party watched helplessly, the chopper roared full throttle and lifted straight up into the air in a cloud of dust. It hovered for a moment, then swept up and away, barely clearing the edge of the canyon as it vanished toward the south!

On the ground, the searchers stared dumbfounded at the sky.

"They . . . they're gone," Uncle Titus said in disbelief.

"You let them escape again!" Aunt Mathilda raged. "Men! Now how do you plan to rescue my nephew?"

"Back to the cars!" the sheriff shouted. "Get word out on the radio. The helicopter was heading south."

The deputies headed back to the trail at a run.

"Wait, sir," Bob cried. "I didn't see Jupiter with them! Just the two kidnappers and a pilot!"

"Maybe we scared them!" Pete exclaimed. "Maybe they left Jupe in that cabin!"

Chief Reynolds turned and led the rush to the cabin. He flung the door open, and everyone hurried inside. They looked all around the single bare room.

"He's not here!" Pete groaned.

"He must have been in the helicopter already," Bob said in dismay. "We were just too late."

"*No, Records,*" a ghostly voice from nowhere said,

"as a matter of fact, you were just in time."

Two floorboards rose up at the rear of the cabin, and a grinning Jupiter emerged from under the floor!

"Jupiter!" everyone cried at once.

"Of course," the stout boy said blandly. "Were you expecting someone else?"

6

Jupiter Finds a Clue

". . . So there was no way out of that cabin," Jupiter explained to the newspaper reporters clustered around him at police headquarters. "But I realized that since there was also nowhere in the cabin to hide, I might make them *think* I'd managed to escape if I just hid under the floor! And it worked! Of course, they might have guessed the truth in time, but when everyone else arrived they had to run."

"Pretty smart for a kid," a reporter said.

"Jupiter Jones," Chief Reynolds pointed out, "isn't an ordinary boy. None of The Three Investigators is ordinary. They are authentic junior detectives, and often help us in our work."

"That's a great story, Chief," the reporter said, and nodded to his photographer. "Get some good pictures, Joe. We'll make the late edition."

While the reporters interviewed him, Jupiter studied the police mug book, which contained photographs of all the people that the Rocky Beach police had ever arrested. He also gave a description of the two kidnappers to a police artist, who made a drawing of each suspect.

"The kidnappers never said what they wanted?" a reporter asked.

"That is police business," Chief Reynolds answered.

"But I can tell you this much: Mr. Titus Jones is not a rich man, and neither he nor his nephew knows of any definite reason for the abduction at this time. We expect to learn the reason and capture the kidnappers shortly."

Grudgingly, the reporters finished taking their pictures and left. Jupiter failed to find the kidnappers in the mug book, and he wasn't satisfied with the drawings.

"They're not really much like the kidnappers," Bob agreed.

"Have you learned something new, Chief?" Pete asked eagerly. "You said you expected to catch them soon."

"I'm afraid not, Pete," the chief admitted. "That was just for the newspapers. In a kidnapping it's important not to let the media reveal what you are actually doing."

"That's why you didn't tell them that I'm convinced it was no ordinary kidnapping?" Jupiter wanted to know.

"Yes, Jupiter," the chief said. "The less the kidnappers think we know, the better."

"I see," Jupiter said, and pondered. "For some reason, though, they mistook me for the son of someone important in their country, wherever that is, and I think it's all some kind of revenge, or politics, or even war. They were after a hostage!"

"Perhaps," the chief acknowledged, "but you're safe now, and we'll handle it. The helicopter is being traced, and those drawings will be circulated. I want you to be careful for a few days. By then, I'm sure we'll have those villains. Now, since your aunt and uncle have already left, we'll send you all home in a police car."

Outside in front of police headquarters, while waiting for the police car, Jupiter looked at his watch. He frowned.

"It's getting late, but perhaps we can get someone to take us in the yard truck," the stout leader said almost to himself.

"Where, Jupe?" Pete asked, and then gulped. "No, don't tell me. I don't think I want to know."

"Jupe!" Bob cried. "Look, it's Worthington!"

The tall chauffeur stood beside the gold-plated Rolls-Royce parked at the curb some four cars up the street. The three boys hurried to him.

"You're still here, Worthington!" Jupiter exclaimed.

"I was not properly dismissed, Master Jones," the chauffeur said, "and I wished to be sure you were safe and in good health." His eyes twinkled. "Besides, it occurred to me that there is still more than an hour before five o'clock, and you might possibly wish transportation somewhere."

"We do!" Jupiter declared. He ran over to the police car that had just pulled up for the boys and explained they didn't need a ride after all. Then he ran cheerfully back to the Rolls-Royce. "Inside, fellows!"

The boys piled into the gleaming vehicle, and Worthington looked back solemnly from the driver's seat. "Where to, sir?"

"Why, back to that box canyon near Rattlesnake Road, of course."

"Oh, no," Pete moaned. "The chief said we were supposed to be careful."

"And we will be," Jupiter said with a grin. "Drive on, Worthington!"

The summer sun was still high when they reached the hidden trail off Rattlesnake Road. Worthington locked the Rolls-Royce, and some twenty-five minutes later they all emerged into the canyon where Jupe had been held captive.

"Since I was in the cabin and wouldn't have a fresh eye for any clues that might be there, I think Pete and Worthington should search in and around it," Jupiter decided. "Bob and I will search the area where the helicopter landed."

"What exactly are we looking for, First?" Bob asked.

"Besides trouble, that is," Pete muttered.

"Any clue at all, Records," Jupiter said, ignoring Pete. "A clue to who the kidnappers are, or where they come from, or what they really want, or where they might be now."

As the sun slowly went down behind the mountain cliffs and plunged the narrow canyon into long shadows, Pete and Worthington searched all around the cabin, without results. Bob and Jupiter did no better out where the helicopter had been. Then Jupiter remembered that the kidnappers had searched for him beyond the cabin. The Investigators and Worthington fanned out and started to work their way down to the end of the canyon. They were growing more and more discouraged when Jupiter suddenly bent over. He picked up something and stared at it. The others ran to him.

"What's that?" Bob asked.

"I'm not sure," Jupiter replied slowly. "Look."

The tiny object glittered in his hand in the final light of the canyon sun. It was a miniature elephant tusk made of what looked like real ivory, set in a gold mesh, and attached to a small gold loop.

"An earring, maybe?" Pete suggested.

"A watch charm or amulet?" Bob speculated. "Possibly

some kind of lucky piece, First?"

"Whatever it is," Jupiter said, "the setting is quite crude and looks handmade. I think it's some kind of foreign handicraft, and not anything you would expect to find in this canyon."

"Do you think that the kidnappers dropped it, First?" Pete asked.

Worthington took the tiny tusk and studied it for a moment. "Now that I think of it, boys, the accents of those kidnappers sounded much like those of people from former British colonies in Africa, and this tusk looks very much like native jewelry made in parts of Africa. So I should venture the opinion that the kidnappers did indeed drop it here."

Jupiter was excited. "Then I think we can find out where they came from!"

"Uh, Jupe," Pete said uneasily, "I thought we were off this case?"

"We can't fool with kidnappers, First," Bob warned.

"No, the police must pursue the kidnappers," the stout First Investigator conceded. "But somewhere I believe there is a boy in danger, and I am convinced that he is in Rocky Beach. It's up to us to find him and help him."

"I should have known you'd find an angle!" Pete said with a sigh.

"He may not even be aware of his danger, Second. At least we can warn him," Jupiter said firmly, and turned to Worthington. "You may drive us home now, Worthington, and then you may return the car to the agency."

"Very good, Master Jones," the chauffeur said.

As they returned to the narrow trail and walked in the fading light toward Rattlesnake Road, Pete frowned.

"Just how do we find this kid?" he wanted to know.

"There are many ways, Second," Jupiter declared confidently. "But before we can find him, we must know more about him. Tonight I will do some research, and we'll meet at Headquarters tomorrow to plan our strategy!"

7

Friends or Enemies?

"Peter! Don't gobble your breakfast," Mrs. Crenshaw said the next morning.

"Sorry, Mom. I'm in kind of a hurry."

Mr. Crenshaw looked up over his newspaper.

"Nothing to do with the kidnapping of your friend Jupiter, I hope," Mr. Crenshaw said seriously. "That's nothing for you boys to mess with."

"No, sir, we know that. We aren't going anywhere near those kidnappers if we can help it."

Mrs. Crenshaw smiled. "It's hard to imagine anyone mistaking Jupiter Jones for someone else. I wouldn't have thought there could be anyone else quite like Jupiter."

"Well, Jupe didn't say anything to them, Mom. I mean, he kept his mouth shut."

"Oh, I see." Mrs. Crenshaw laughed. "That would make a difference with Jupiter, wouldn't it?"

Pete grinned in response. He finished his breakfast, then rushed out to his bike. The air was still cool as he rode to the salvage yard and stopped by the back fence fifty yards from the corner. The entire fence had been decorated by Rocky Beach artists, and here in the rear was a dramatic scene of the San Francisco fire of 1906.

ete removed the eye of a little dog painted into the scene—the eye was a knot in the wood—and reached inside the fence. He released a catch, three boards swung up, and he went into the yard through Red Gate Rover.

He went on across the salvage yard through the mounds of junk, and found Jupiter at work in his outdoor workshop. The leader of the detective team had parts of three small instruments spread all over the workbench.

"Our emergency signals need a lot of adjustments," Jupiter said. "You can help me while we wait for Bob."

"What about your research, and the plans to find that Ian kid?" Pete asked as he bent over the scattered parts of the emergency signals, which Jupiter had built for their work many years ago. "Didn't you find out anything?"

"I wouldn't say that," Jupiter said, grinning. "As a matter of fact, I found out a great deal last night. I don't think it will be too difficult a task to locate Ian Carew!"

"Tell me!" Pete cried.

"We'll wait for Bob," Jupiter said maddeningly. "No sense in going over it all twice."

Pete fumed in frustration, but Jupiter only grinned and continued to work on the emergency signals. The two boys had all the parts cleaned and readjusted and ready for reassembly by the time Bob arrived. He came bursting into the workshop through Green Gate One—two loose green boards in the front fence of the junkyard.

"Sorry," he said, out of breath from riding his bike so fast, "Mom grabbed me for some jobs around the house. What are our plans, Jupe? Have you heard anything more from Chief Reynolds?"

"Yes," Jupiter replied, "I called the chief earlier this

morning. They found the helicopter abandoned in a field up near Ventura."

"You mean they fooled us? Turned north after heading south?" Bob exclaimed.

Jupiter nodded. "A logical move once they knew they had been spotted by the police. Chief Reynolds said there were no clues in the aircraft, and it had been rented and paid for by mail. When the pilot arrived at the airfield, he was already wearing those flying clothes and goggles so no one could describe him. Of course, his pilot's papers were fakes, and the name and address he gave turned out to be phony."

"So that's a lot of help," Pete grumbled.

"What about the kidnappers?" Bob asked.

"No one's even been able to identify them yet, much less apprehend them," Jupiter said. "The fingerprints that the police found in the helicopter and the Mercedes aren't on file with the FBI in Washington. And the Mercedes turned out to be rented, too."

"You mean we're getting nowhere," Pete said bluntly.

"Not exactly, Second." Jupiter smiled. "As I said, I spent last night doing research, and I think we can—"

Before he could finish what he was going to say, a forceful voice boomed out behind him.

"So there you are, Jupiter Jones!" Aunt Mathilda stood in the workshop entrance, glaring at Jupiter with her hands on her hips. "You did promise to finish cleaning out the small storeroom two days ago, didn't you? I did let you off yesterday against my better judgment, didn't I? Then you did promise faithfully to get to work first thing this morning, didn't you?"

"I'm sorry, Aunt Mathilda," Jupiter said sheepishly.

"You should be! I suppose it's all because it's the last week before school opens. Running off, lazing around, eating everything in sight. My refrigerator looks like the buzzards have been at it!"

"I–I haven't touched—" Jupiter stammered.

"Stuff and nonsense. Look at you, getting fatter all the time. Some work will do you good!"

"But," Pete and Bob protested, "we've got something—"

"Whatever it is, it can wait, and you two can just put this workshop into some order while Jupiter finishes the job he started. Now march, young man!"

Jupiter sighed. "Put the signals back together, fellows. I won't be too long."

"If he doesn't stop for too many snacks," Aunt Mathilda said sarcastically.

Bob and Pete nodded glumly as Jupiter marched away toward the yard office, with Aunt Mathilda stepping behind him like a Marine Corps drill sergeant. Burning with curiosity about what Jupiter had been going to say, they went to work reassembling the three emergency signals. It was slow, delicate work, and Pete was all thumbs. But with the help of the defter Bob, they finally got the small instruments back together.

After that they straightened up the workshop.

When Jupiter still hadn't returned, they started to crawl into Tunnel Two to wait inside Headquarters.

"Hold it, fellows!"

Red-faced and sweating from his exertions in the small storeroom, Jupiter hurried into the workshop. Bob and Pete clambered back out of the tunnel.

"What about last night, Jupe?" Pete demanded eagerly.

"What did you find out?" Bob asked.

"Well, I looked up—"

"JUPITER JONES!"

It was Aunt Mathilda calling again from near the office.

"Oh, no!" Pete groaned.

"Let's hide!" Bob urged.

"I'm afraid that wouldn't help," Jupiter said.

"Jupe's right," Pete agreed hopelessly. "You can't hide from Aunt Mathilda. She's Scotland Yard, the FBI, and the Canadian Mounties combined! We might as well go out."

They left the workshop and started across the salvage yard, threading their way past the mounds of junk. Bob suddenly pointed ahead to Aunt Mathilda, who stood outside the yard office.

"Jupe! There're two men with her!"

"N-not the kidnappers!" Pete stammered.

"No," Bob said, "one of them's black."

"Black?" Jupiter exclaimed. "Of course, that would be logical. Come on, fellows."

"Logical?" Pete said. "What do you mean, logical?"

But Jupiter was already walking ahead. Bob and Pete caught up to him as they reached the office. Aunt Mathilda eyed the boys suspiciously.

"These men say they want to talk to you three," she said. "Something about hiring you. I hope it's not some scheme you all cooked up to get out of work the rest of the week!"

"No, madam," one of the strangers said. He was tall and blond and as sunburned as the kidnappers. "We have a small investigation for the boys."

The Three Investigators stared at the tall, blond man

—he had the same odd British accent as the kidnappers!

"It had better be small," Aunt Mathilda snapped. "They start school again next week, and about time too."

With that parting shot, Aunt Mathilda strode off into the office, leaving the boys with the two strangers. Jupiter looked quickly around, then motioned for the two men to follow the boys back to the workshop. Once there, Jupiter turned eagerly to the two men.

"It's about the kidnapping, isn't it?" he said. "Who are you gentlemen?"

"I am Gordon MacKenzie," the blond man said, "and this"—he nodded to the black man—"is Adam Ndula. And, yes, it's about your kidnapping."

"We need the help of good local detectives," Adam Ndula said. "We can tell you why you were kidnapped, and what the kidnappers were really after."

"We'll be glad to help, Mr. Ndula," Jupiter said. "But we already know why I was kidnapped, and what the kidnappers really want!"

"We do?" Pete said.

"Yes, Second, we do," Jupiter declared smugly. "I was kidnapped because I look a lot like a boy named Ian Carew. Ian is the son of Sir Roger Carew. Sir Roger is prime minister of the small British colony of Nanda in southern Africa, and is preparing Nanda to become an independent country next year with government by the black majority and the Nanda-born moderate whites. But he is opposed both by the underground Black Nandan Alliance, whose members want to expel all whites from the country, and the white extremists of the National Party, who want an all-white government and army to keep the black majority in near slavery."

"Wow, Jupe how do you know all that?" Bob wondered.

"What's it got to do with the kidnapping?" Pete added.

"It's the reason for the kidnapping, Second," the stout leader declared. "The kidnappers belong to the white extremist National Party. They planned to kidnap Ian Carew to hold him as a hostage and force Sir Roger to change his plans and keep Nanda under all-white rule. Mr. MacKenzie and Mr. Ndula are members of Sir Roger's moderate party who have come to try to save Ian."

The workshop became suddenly quiet.

"You know a great deal," Adam Ndula said. "I think too much!"

He held an enormous pistol in his hand.

8

"In Djanga's Place"

Ndula's eyes narrowed suspiciously. He held the pistol aimed straight at Jupiter.

"There is only one way you could know all that," the grim Nandan said. "Only one way you could know who we are. You are working with those kidnappers! You are a spy!"

"Easy, Adam," MacKenzie said. His voice was quiet, but his eyes were as deadly as Ndula's. "Well, young man, what do you have to say? How do you know so much about us?"

"It's really all quite simple, Mr. MacKenzie," Jupiter said in his most dignified voice. "I am neither a spy nor a fool. If I had been working with the kidnappers, I wouldn't have been so foolish as to reveal myself."

Ndula watched him closely. "Go on, boy."

"Explain how it is all so simple," MacKenzie said.

"Very well," Jupiter replied. "In the first place, while I was a prisoner I *listened* to the kidnappers. They had strange accents, and had obviously mistaken me for a boy named Ian who was the son of an important man named Sir Roger. After I escaped, we went back to where I had been held. We found this—" He held up the tiny ivory tusk with its gold setting. "Our chauffeur,

Worthington, was sure it was from Africa, and was also
convinced that the accent of the kidnappers was that of
people from some British colony in Africa."

MacKenzie took the tiny tusk and studied it. He held
it up for Ndula to see. Ndula shook his head.

"We have an excellent library in Rocky Beach," Jupiter
continued. "It didn't take me long to discover that the
British colony of Nanda has a prime minister named Sir
Roger Carew, and is in the middle of a struggle for independence. The kidnappers were clearly enemies of Sir
Roger planning to hold Ian as a weapon against him, so
they had to be white extremists opposed to his plans for
Nanda's future. Since you two have the same accents,
and since you are each of a different race but working
together, it was a simple deduction that you are followers
of Sir Roger Carew!"

"Gee," Pete exclaimed, "it *is* pretty simple."

"When young Jones explains it," MacKenzie said, smiling. He glanced at Ndula. "Satisfied, Adam?"

"Yes," Ndula said, and put his pistol back into its
shoulder holster. "The boys seem to be honest."

"And good detectives," MacKenzie said. "Which I
think was what young Jones intended to show us, eh?"

Jupiter flushed and grinned. "I thought maybe a demonstration of our work would help."

"Yes, very good," MacKenzie said. "We arrived in
Rocky Beach only yesterday, and read of your kidnapping in the evening newspaper. When we saw your picture, we knew at once what had happened. The paper
mentioned your connection with The Three Investigators, so this morning we made inquiries and found
that you boys truly are detectives. But a demonstration

is better than words, eh?"

Jupiter nodded, and presented the Investigators' business card with a flourish. The two Nandans studied it. It read:

THE THREE INVESTIGATORS
"We Investigate Anything"
?   ?   ?
First Investigator .... Jupiter Jones
Second Investigator .... Peter Crenshaw
Records and Research .... Bob Andrews

"Very professional," commented MacKenzie.

"Then you'll hire us!" Pete cried.

MacKenzie nodded to Ndula. "What do you think, Adam? Are these resourceful young men what we need?"

"I think they will do, Gordon," Ndula said with a grin.

Bob and Pete beamed, and Jupiter looked thoughtful.

"Sir, just how much do I resemble Ian Carew?" he asked.

"Call me Mac, and I'll call you Jupiter, eh? You're Ian's double—the resemblance is uncanny. Not perfect to someone who knows Ian well, but amazingly similar. Then, Ian has been in the United States for the last two years, and a boy changes quite a lot in that amount of time, so those kidnappers could easily mistake you for him. Of course, Ian has a Nandan accent. I'm a bit surprised—"

"I guessed that, Mac," Jupiter explained, "so I made sure that I said nothing. I was afraid that if the kidnappers discovered their mistake, I would be in greater danger."

"So you would have been," Ndula said grimly. "From their names and descriptions we don't know them, but all those white extremists are very dangerous."

"We think they dropped that little tusk," Bob said. "Does it mean anything to you?"

"No," Ndula said, "but it is definitely from Nanda."

"Then there's no doubt that the kidnappers are Nandan extremists?" Jupiter said.

"None at all," MacKenzie declared. "Ian has been going to school in Los Angeles to prevent just such an attempt to use him to blackmail Sir Roger. Somehow the extremists discovered Ian's whereabouts, and tried to abduct him in Los Angeles a week ago. He escaped, but vanished. At home Sir Roger was frantic until Ian sent a message through the Nandan Trade Mission in Los Angeles."

"What message?" Jupiter said.

"What's a trade mission?" Pete wanted to know.

"A trade mission is an official group that tries to increase business between two countries," Ndula explained.

"And the message was short and puzzling," MacKenzie said. "Almost meaningless to us, except that it mentioned Rocky Beach. Ian must have been afraid that our enemies would see the message, and obviously they did or they wouldn't have come here looking."

"You want us to try to decipher it!" Pete exclaimed.

"Let's see it!" Bob cried.

"It is at our hotel, in the hotel safe for security," Ndula said. "We will take you there at once."

The three boys followed the Nandans out of the salvage yard to a long, black Cadillac. As they all climbed inside, Pete suddenly stopped.

"Jupe!" the tall Second Investigator said urgently. "The vacant lot!"

He pointed across the street to the vacant lot next to Aunt Mathilda and Uncle Titus's house.

"Someone was there by the front clump of bushes!" Pete said. "I'm sure of it!"

"Shall we see?" MacKenzie said.

They approached the lot warily. It was well screened by bushes near the street, but looking past the shrubbery they could see all the way through to the next block. There was no one in the lot. Pete searched around the bushes where he thought he'd seen someone, and pointed to the ground. A discarded cigarette butt lay there, still smoldering.

"Someone *was* here!" Pete cried.

"Possibly just a workman taking a smoking break," Jupiter said uneasily.

"Perhaps," MacKenzie said.

"After all," added Jupe, as if trying to convince himself, "why would anyone be spying on the salvage yard? If the kidnappers are still in the area, they must have seen the newspaper and realized their mistake."

They returned to the Cadillac. Ndula drove, and MacKenzie turned to the boys.

"We must find Ian, and quickly," he said. "Perhaps no one was watching you from that vacant lot, but I fear the kidnappers are still near Rocky Beach. They won't give up easily. They have too much at stake in Nanda to be scared off by the police."

"People will do almost anything for what they believe in," Jupiter agreed ominously.

"Yes, Jupiter," MacKenzie said. "And not just political

extremists. Sir Roger loves Ian, boys, but his country comes first. Even if the extremists capture Ian, Sir Roger will not do what they want. Not even for Ian's life."

The three boys gulped, but said nothing. Soon the big car turned into the drive of the Miramar Hotel on the beach. MacKenzie took the boys up to the Nandans' room while Ndula got the message from the hotel safe. MacKenzie locked the door behind Ndula, and they all crowded around as Jupiter read the message aloud.

" '*Attacked in L.A. Scared. Rocky Beach. Djanga's place.*' "

The boys looked at each other in dismay.

Pete exclaimed, "He hardly says anything!"

"And there's nothing that seems to be in code," Bob added.

"No," Jupiter agreed, staring at the cryptic message. "Except perhaps that last phrase—*Djanga's place*. What does that mean?"

"We hoped you could tell us," MacKenzie said. "We've looked in every guidebook on Rocky Beach, but there's no reference to Djanga. We thought it must be something very local, known only to people who live here."

"I never heard of it," Bob said.

"Me, neither," Pete agreed.

Jupiter only shook his head.

"It is hopeless, Gordon," Ndula said, his shoulders sagging. "These boys cannot help us after all."

9

Jupiter Stands Firm

"Nothing," Jupiter said firmly, "is ever hopeless."

"You have an idea, Jupiter?" MacKenzie said quickly.

"What is it, First?" Bob asked.

Jupiter pondered the brief and puzzling message.

"Ian was scared by the attempt to abduct him in Los Angeles," the stocky leader said. "He ran away, and came up here. Why did he pick Rocky Beach to hide out in?"

"He'd come here on vacations from school," Ndula said. "When Sir Roger visited him last year, they spent a week up here."

"Then he *knew* Rocky Beach," Jupiter exclaimed.

"Sure he did, he came here," Pete said. "Why is that anything special?"

"It's special, Pete, because it probably means that he had some definite place where he planned to hide, and wanted to tell Sir Roger where he'd be. That's what he must have been trying to do when he used the words *Djanga's place*."

"But," Ndula objected, "Sir Roger has no idea what Ian meant by that."

"Nevertheless," Jupiter insisted, "it must be the clue to where he's hiding. He was frightened and running, and

56

he wouldn't have wasted words in his message. There must be a good reason why he used *Djanga's place,* and since there doesn't seem to be anyplace in Rocky Beach with that name, and we've never heard of anything like it, it must have some *indirect* meaning! It must be intended to give a *clue* to his location."

"So the extremists wouldn't understand it if they saw his message," Pete exclaimed.

"Precisely, Second," Jupiter said. "Mac, the word is obviously African. What does it mean in Nandan?"

"That's just the trouble," MacKenzie said unhappily. "It doesn't mean anything helpful. Djanga is the name of the last great leader of the Nanda tribe who make up the majority of our native people. Adam is a member of the mind almost at once. Mac, can you tell us the most important places, events, or actions connected with Djanga? Something most people from Nanda would know?"

"Well—" MacKenzie thought hard. "There's his great victory over the British Army at Imbala, and his final defeat at Zingwala. The general he defeated was Lord Fernwood, and the one who beat him in the end was General Audley."

Bob whipped out his pocket notebook and began writing down all the names.

"Djanga's capital was Ulaga," Ndula added. "After he was defeated the British imprisoned him at Fort George."

"He escaped and tried to fight again," MacKenzie continued. "His headquarters then _____ ____ Karga tribe himself."

"Djanga was the last chief who battled against the European invaders and settlers, in the early 1880s," Ndula explained. "His name means something like 'thunder cloud' or 'rain noise,' depending on how it is translated."

"That's all?" Jupiter said, disappointed. "All right, is there some special *place* he had? Or some particular event, or action, or person associated with him?"

"There must be hundreds, Jupiter," MacKenzie said. "Djanga is a legend in Nanda. There are endless myths, stories, battles, people, and events associated with him. It could take weeks to try to research them all."

"And we don't have weeks," Ndula said. "Time is vital. We may not have even days."

"Gosh, Jupe, it looks pretty hopeless," Bob said.

"There must be a way!" Jupiter fumed. "Ian was desperate, so he would have used an association that was well known. Something that he was sure would come to

"And he died in a final little skirmish near a village named Smith's Ford," Ndula concluded.

Jupiter nodded. "What we must do is take all the names connected with him, and—"

A loud knocking on the door made them all whirl. The knocking was sharp and urgent. A woman's voice called out.

"Mr. MacKenzie? Mr. Ndula? Are you in there?"

MacKenzie strode to the door. "It's Miss Lessing from the trade mission. She's our contact with Sir Roger."

"Perhaps Sir Roger has found Ian!" Ndula cried.

MacKenzie unlocked the door, and a tall, dark-haired woman in a navy sweater and gray slacks walked in hastily.

"Have you found him?" she asked quickly. "You told me not to use the telephone, and there's an urgent secret communiqué from Sir Roger saying—"

Miss Lessing suddenly saw the boys, and stopped speaking. She stared at them suspiciously.

"I didn't realize you weren't alone, Mr. MacKenzie," she said stiffly. "I'm afraid Sir Roger's message is official state business. I can't reveal it to strangers."

"Is it about Ian, Miss Lessing?" MacKenzie asked.

"Has Sir Roger found him? Or heard from him again?" Ndula added.

"No, I'm afraid not either."

"All right," MacKenzie said. "Boys, I think you can begin your research at once. Remember, we must find Ian as soon as possible. Contact us here the instant you come up with anything at all."

The boys nodded, and left the hotel room. Once outside they hurried down the hotel driveway to a bus stop.

"Where do we start investigating, First?" Bob asked eagerly.

"We compare everything we know about Djanga against the telephone book, city directory, city maps, and any other references to places in Rocky Beach where Ian might hide," Jupiter instructed. "He wrote Djanga's *place*, so we'll start with the places, and we'll split up. Pete can go to City Hall to check maps, Bob can study the city directory and telephone book, and I'll try the Historical Society."

"Can I go home for lunch first?" Pete asked with a grin.

"Knock it off, Second," Jupiter said, sighing. "Grab a hot dog somewhere, and then start on the maps. We'll all meet at Headquarters later this afternoon."

The bus came, and they got on. While they rode into downtown Rocky Beach, Bob took out his pocket notebook and made three lists of all the places Djanga had been associated with. Armed with the lists, the boys split up for their separate investigations.

It was past three-thirty when Jupiter left the Historical Society and headed for the Investigators' secret headquarters. He had found nothing in any local guidebooks or recent histories of the Rocky Beach area that sounded anything like Imbala, or Zingwala, or Ulaga, or Fort George, or the Karga Valley, or Smith's Ford, or even Fernwood or Audley.

Neither Bob nor Pete was at Headquarters. Jupe put new batteries into the emergency signals on the outdoor workbench, and did some fine tuning on the instruments. Then he crawled into the trailer room and sat trying to think of *some* connection between Chief Djanga and Rocky Beach.

There had to be an answer, and Jupiter was sure it was in one of the famous places associated with the old chief. Ian wouldn't have wanted his clue to be *too* hard to figure out.

It was nearly five o'clock before Bob and Pete finally arrived. Their glum faces told the story.

"Nothing at all," Bob said, sighing.

"They're mostly all African names, First," Pete added. "Rocky Beach just doesn't have anything African in it."

"We haven't tried everywhere," Jupiter said. "After dinner we'll go to the library and look up Djanga. Maybe there are some other important place names that Mac and Ndula forgot to tell us about."

"I'm going out with my folks tonight," Bob told him.

"And I've got chores after dinner," Pete said.

"Very well," Jupiter replied. "I shall continue alone."

"Jupe?" Pete said unhappily. "I've got this feeling that we're on the wrong track."

"Maybe he's right, Jupe," Bob said.

"No! I'm convinced Ian was telling us where he is." But Jupiter didn't look so confident now.

10

Jupiter Misses Something

Jupiter toyed with his breakfast the next morning. He didn't feel very hungry.

"My stars! Are you sick, boy?" Aunt Mathilda boomed.

"No, ma'am," Jupiter said, and sighed.

He had slept little, awakened early, and had lain in bed in the cool dawn wondering if Pete was perhaps right this time. He had found a whole book about Nanda in the library, had checked it out, and had spent half the night reading it in Headquarters. It had added nothing important that he could see to the names and places Mac-Kenzie and Ndula had given the Investigators.

"What about some bacon? A waffle?" Aunt Mathilda suggested, suddenly concerned, as Jupiter finally finished his cereal.

"Well, maybe one waffle," he agreed. "And just a little bacon. Four or five pieces, that's all."

"The boy's going to starve away," Uncle Titus said.

Jupiter was still certain that Ian Carew had been trying to reveal where he was hiding, but either Ian had been too careful, or Jupe was missing something. For once he had to admit he was stumped. And worse—as he finished his breakfast he couldn't think of anything to do next!

Just then the telephone rang. Jupiter didn't even look up from his last piece of bacon. He was brooding about his failure. He hated the thought that he could ever be beaten.

"It's Bob for you," Aunt Mathilda said.

Jupiter took the receiver wearily. "Yes, Records?"

"You found it, First! Why didn't you call us?"

"What?" Jupiter said, blinking. "What did I find?"

"Why, the answer! Where Ian is hiding!"

"Don't joke, Records," Jupiter said angrily. "I'm not feeling very humorous this morning. We'll just have to go to MacKenzie and Ndula and try some other way. Maybe—"

"You mean you didn't spot it?" Bob sounded amazed.

"Spot it? Spot what? Where?"

"In the book you got from the library last night."

"What are you talking about? There's nothing new in that book. I read it thoroughly."

"Then you missed it! We're both over here in Headquarters. Hurry!"

"Bob? What—?"

But Bob had hung up. Jupiter gulped the last bite of waffle, and hurried out of the house and across the street to the salvage yard. When he emerged through the trap door into Headquarters, Pete and Bob grinned maddeningly at him.

"A detective has to keep his eyes open at all times," Pete said with mock seriousness.

"Did you really miss it, First?" Bob chortled.

"If there was really anything to miss," Jupiter muttered.

"Tell him, Records," Pete urged.

"Well," Bob began, "you weren't here when we arrived, and while we waited Pete noticed the book you got last night. So we looked at the part about Chief Djanga, and there it was!"

"There *what* was?" Jupiter demanded. "Get to the point, Records."

Bob picked up the book and began to read. " 'For Djanga, the last of the great Nandan chiefs, the great moment of hope came when his superb regiments defeated and wiped out a poorly commanded British force of six hundred regulars and one thousand native troops at Imbala, the Hill of the Red Lion, thus halting the European advance for at least three years.' "

Bob stopped. Both he and Pete smiled eagerly at Jupiter. The stocky leader of the team blinked at them.

"So?" he said, waiting. "We already knew about Imbala—"

"Jupe!" Bob cried. "The Hill of the Red Lion! The meaning of Imbala in English! Don't you remember? The Red Lion Ranch! The famous old hotel where all the Hollywood stars used to come to vacation in privacy!"

For a moment Jupiter seemed stunned. Then he laughed aloud, and clapped Bob on the back.

"You've done it, Records!" he exclaimed. "The Red Lion Ranch! It's not so well known today, but it's still quiet and secluded, and just the sort of place where Sir Roger Carew would take his son on vacation! I missed that meaning of Imbala completely!"

"We all make mistakes," Pete said innocently.

He and Bob burst out laughing, and Jupiter finally joined in.

"All right, all right," Jupiter said ruefully. "Now let's

call MacKenzie and Ndula!"

But no one answered in the Nandans' room when Jupe called their hotel.

"They're probably having breakfast," announced Jupe. "Let's go over there and find them."

"We'd better take the bus," Bob said. "They'll probably drive us up to the Red Lion, and our bikes would be in the way."

"Good idea," Pete agreed.

Jupiter nodded, and the boys rushed out of Headquarters. Twenty minutes later, a bus deposited them by the Miramar Hotel. At the front desk the clerk called the Nandans' room, and was told to send the boys right up.

"Have you heard anything?" Jupiter asked as the boys entered the room.

"No, only that a critical situation is about to develop in Nanda," MacKenzie said, "and Sir Roger is desperate that we find Ian."

"I think we may be able to help you do that," Jupiter said triumphantly, and told MacKenzie and Ndula what they had discovered.

"The Hill of the Red Lion! Of course!" Ndula exclaimed. "That is just what Imbala means. Good work, boys. You must be correct. Sir Roger was too upset to see what Ian was trying to tell him!"

"I told you they were smart boys." MacKenzie beamed. "We'll get the car."

Down in the parking lot they all got into the big Cadillac, and MacKenzie drove off. Bob directed him through the town to the northern outskirts in the foothills. All but invisible from the road, the Red Lion Ranch consisted of a three-story main building and a cluster of small yellow stucco buildings and white frame cottages behind a high hedge of oleander and hibiscus. Mac-Kenzie parked, and they went into the main building.

At the registration desk a clerk in an immaculate black suit looked up with a polite smile. Then his smile faded as he saw them.

"Mr. Ember!" the clerk cried.

A door behind the desk opened, and a short, thin little man in a checked sportscoat and brown slacks came out. The short man glared at Jupiter the instant he saw him.

"So you're back! It's about time, and you can just pay your bill at once, young man!"

"Then Ian Carew *was* here!" Jupiter exclaimed.

"Are you the manager?" MacKenzie said to the short man.

"Yes, I am the manager," the short man snapped, and went on glaring at Jupiter. "I don't know what you're up to, young man, but if you don't pay your bill at once I shall be forced to contact the police!"

"That will not be necessary," Ndula said quietly. "We will settle the bill. This young man is not Ian Carew."

"Not?" The manager stared at them, confused and suspicious. "Don't you think I can see—"

"He looks like Ian," MacKenzie said, "but we assure you he is not," and he explained the resemblance of the two boys.

"Perhaps you saw my picture in the paper the other day," Jupiter added, eager to prove who he was.

The manager shook his head. "We've been extremely busy this week hosting a small conference. I haven't had a moment to look at a paper." He stared hard at Jupiter, noting his casual, baggy clothing. "I must say," he added with a sniff, "that I've never seen Ian Carew dressed quite so . . . informally. But if you aren't Ian, why should these men offer to pay his bill?"

"Mr. Ndula and I are representatives of Sir Roger Carew," explained MacKenzie. "Here are our credentials. You may check them with our trade mission in Los Angeles. Now, if you will tell us what Ian owes you, we will pay you."

The clerk handed a bill to Ndula, who paid it while the manager studied the Nandans' credentials and shook his head.

"This is most confusing," the manager said.

"I realize that, and I wish we could explain more," MacKenzie said, "but it is a delicate matter, and extremely urgent. We must find Ian at once if he isn't here. Can you tell us everything that happened since he arrived?"

"Well—" The manager hesitated, and then nodded. "Very well. He arrived about a week or so ago. I recognized him from his previous stay with his father, of course. He said that he was to meet Sir Roger here in a few days. Naturally, we granted him every courtesy. But a few days later two other men came here for him. They also claimed to be from Sir Roger. They appeared to know the boy quite well, and asked his room number. We do not give out that information without first announcing the visitors. I asked them their names, and called young Carew's room. He told me to send them right up."

"Can you describe the men?" Jupiter asked quickly.

"Not very well—they came four days ago. But one was

quite stocky with curly brown hair, and the other was much taller and thinner with dark hair. I don't recall their names."

MacKenzie and Ndula glanced at Jupiter. He nodded. The men sounded like the two kidnappers.

"What happened after they went up?" MacKenzie asked.

"It was rather odd, although I thought nothing of it at the time. Quite soon after the men went up, I saw young Carew leave the hotel through the main entrance. Perhaps five minutes later the two men came down and ran out also."

"And that's the last time you saw Ian?" Ndula said.

"Indeed it was! Young Carew never returned, leaving his bill unpaid!"

"Then we've lost him again," Ndula said bitterly.

"Gosh, I was so sure we'd found him," Bob wailed.

Jupiter looked thoughtful. "May we see his room?"

The manager glanced toward the key boxes. "Very well, it appears to be unoccupied now." He reached for the key. "Room twenty-nine, second floor at the front. You can take the elevator on your right, or the stairs just beyond the elevator."

As they moved toward the elevator, MacKenzie shook his head doubtfully.

"Why look at the room, Jupiter? He's not there. All we can do now is hope that he gets in touch with us again."

"He was clearly suspicious of those men," Jupiter said, pressing the elevator button, "or he wouldn't have run from the hotel. He must have recognized them as the men who had tried to abduct him before. Somehow he escaped them again—probably before they got to his room."

"How does that help us?" Ndula asked.

"He expected his message to bring Sir Roger to this hotel," Jupiter explained. "When he had to flee again, he would have wanted help to follow, so I'm hoping that he left some message telling where he planned to go next."

The elevator came, and they all got on. Jupiter pressed the button for the second floor.

"Since the only place that Ian could have been sure anyone would look is his room, any message will be there!"

11

A Clever Fugitive

As they unlocked the door and stepped into room twenty-nine, Pete groaned.

"Jupe, the whole room's been cleaned!"

Nodding uneasily, Jupiter glanced slowly around the large room. Sunlight streamed in through high windows, which looked out over the driveway and taxi stand in front of the hotel, and then across the outskirts of Rocky Beach to the blue Pacific Ocean.

"Anything he left is probably gone!" Bob wailed.

"They're right, Jupiter," MacKenzie agreed. "Any note would have been thrown away by the maid."

"Probably," Jupiter admitted, "although hotel maids don't always clean too well. But I don't think Ian would have left an ordinary note anyway. There was too great a chance that the kidnappers would search his room, either immediately or later on. No, Ian probably left something deceptive, a kind of code or symbol. Something that Sir Roger's helpers would recognize but not the enemy. It might be on a piece of paper, or it might not."

"You mean," Bob concluded, "something that he could have arranged quickly, that wouldn't be removed when the room was cleaned, that the kidnappers wouldn't notice in a search, and that his friends would probably spot."

"Exactly, Records."

"Then let's find it!" MacKenzie said.

While Pete searched the bathroom, the others combed the bedroom. They looked high and low, turning over everything, looking behind pictures and drapes and under rugs. They tried under the heating grilles and in the ceiling light fixture. Jupe even pulled the bedding off to see if Ian had written on the fiber-content tag on the mattress. But no one found anything that looked like a message or a clue.

"We're probably being too direct again," Jupiter decided. "In his first message Ian used a double code: Djanga's place meant Imbala, and then Imbala meant the Red Lion. The clue was twice removed from the message."

"And it could only be solved by someone with special knowledge," Bob pointed out.

"Right. So anyone who tracked Ian this far would know certain things. I'm sure Ian was counting on that," Jupiter declared. "Mac, does Ian have any special habits, interests, or peculiarities?"

"He's interested in Nandan history," Ndula said.

"And he collects African wood carvings," MacKenzie added, "and, wait, he draws little sketches. Especially on walls. Sir Roger once said Ian even drew on his executive office walls!"

"A sketch in some spot that wouldn't be cleaned at once, and wouldn't be noticed by the kidnappers," Jupiter exclaimed. "That's what we should look for! Search everywhere again!"

But again they found nothing—no drawings, no marks at all on any wall or piece of furniture.

"There's nothing here, Jupe," Pete said with a sigh. "I guess Ian didn't have time after he spotted the kidnappers."

Jupiter whirled toward Pete. "I believe, Second, you've just said it!"

"I did?" Pete replied. "What did I say?"

"Ian is obviously very smart," Jupiter said slowly, "yet he told the manager to send the visitors right up! He was in hiding, and he couldn't have been sure if they were friends or enemies, but he had the manager send them right up. Would we have?"

"No," Bob said. "We'd have had the manager stall them until we could have a secret look at them!"

Jupiter nodded. "Of course, Ian could have seen the men from the window, but that would have been a lucky accident. No, there's only one reason for Ian to have had them come right up—he didn't need to stall them, and perhaps make them realize he was suspicious, because he had a plan all ready!"

"What plan, Jupe?" Bob wanted to know.

"The simplest of all—to leave the room and hide where he could see them, in a place where he would have had a head start in running again if they turned out to be his attackers from Los Angeles. Come on."

The others followed him out of the room and along the corridor.

"Someplace close to the exits," said Jupe, thinking aloud. "Someplace where he could see their faces. Someplace"—his eyes searched the hallway—"like that storage closet!"

It was a long, narrow walk-in closet for linens and mops, only a few feet from the stairway. With the door open an inch, there was a clear view of the elevator and the top of the stairs. Anyone arriving on the floor and heading for Ian's room could be easily seen.

"Look for any kind of pencil drawing!" Jupiter instructed.

Pete found it almost at once, on the inside of the closet door.

"Here! Wow, it's a really good little sketch. A car. I can see the driver, and something like a badge on the side, and something on top!"

Jupiter frowned. "A car? But what could a car mean?"

"It's not a regular car, First!" Bob cried. "Look, the driver has a cap on, and that thing on top is a light! It's a taxi!"

MacKenzie said, "There's a taxi stand out front!"

"He expected us to guess what he'd do to observe any visitors," Ndula said, "and is telling us he planned to flee in a taxi!"

They practically ran outside to the single taxi waiting at the hotel taxi stand. The driver was reading a magazine. No, he hadn't taken any boy from the hotel four days ago or any time.

"How many taxis operate from this stand?" Ndula asked.

"Plenty, mister, but all from our company. Exclusive."

"Where is your main garage?" MacKenzie asked.

Following the driver's directions, MacKenzie drove Ndula and the boys to the central garage and office of the taxi company. It was in an area of railroad tracks and lumber yards not far from the harbor. The group found the day manager in his cluttered office at the rear of the garage. After they had explained what they needed, the manager checked a list.

"The Red Lion? Four days ago? Okay, we had five drivers working out there that day. Let's see, I think Falzone and Johansen are in the shop right now. You can try them."

Johansen was working over the engine of his taxi, and had not taken any boy from the Red Lion four days ago.

Falzone was having a coffee break. "Sure, I took a kid from the Red Lion that day, and that's the kid!" He pointed straight at Jupiter. "You got kidnapped a couple of days later, right? I saw your picture in the paper. Boy, that must have been some scary—"

"I was kidnapped," Jupiter interrupted, "but I'm not the boy you took in your taxi. Look more closely at me."

The taxi man frowned. "Well, you sure look like the same kid. Only you're not dressed the same, and you sound different. So, okay, if you say so—you're somebody else."

"Can you remember where you took the other boy?" Ndula demanded.

"Sure." Falzone nodded. "I remember good because the kid acted funny, like maybe he was up to something. He ran out of the hotel, told me to drive to the other side of town, and kept looking back. I figured maybe he swiped something from the hotel, or was maybe running away. Then this car—"

"But where did you take him?" MacKenzie said impatiently.

"I'm telling you," Falzone said. "He's looking back all the way, and we get all across town, and suddenly he says to stop! It's right in the middle of a block of nothing except warehouses and factories. He pays me off, gets out, and runs off into an alley. He didn't even wait for his change. Then, like I was going to say, this car comes past me going real slow. It didn't stop, but I figure it was after the kid."

"What kind of car?" Jupiter asked.

"Green Mercedes. Real nice. I always wanted one."

"Take us to where you dropped the boy!" Ndula ordered.

"Sure, it ain't far."

It wasn't. On the outskirts of the town, Falzone stopped on a deserted block of warehouses, small manufacturing shops, and vacant lots. The taxi driver pointed to an alley between two buildings.

"He ran off up there. Last I saw of him."

They paid the taxi man, and MacKenzie parked the big Cadillac at the curb.

"Why would he want to come here?" Pete wondered, looking all around at the deserted neighborhood.

"Maybe he just wanted to shake off the kidnappers," Bob said. "He must have realized they were following him."

"That is quite possible, Records," Jupiter agreed. "In which case he would have been seeking a refuge. Let's follow him into that alley, and see if there are further clues."

The alley was narrow, with nothing but bare brick walls on either side. There were three doors, but all were locked with large, rusted padlocks that had not been opened in some time. The five searchers reached the other end of the alley.

"What do we do now?" Pete asked.

The street at this end of the alley was almost exactly like the one they had left. It held nothing but low, silent warehouses, small factories, and vacant lots littered with junk. Nearby, a cross street joined it, forming a T.

"He could have gone in three different directions," Ndula said slowly. "He could be anywhere."

12

The Trail Ends!

"In any direction, yes," Jupiter said, "but not anywhere."

"What do you mean, Jupe?" Bob wanted to know.

"The kidnappers were close behind him, and he knew it," Jupiter pointed out. "I don't believe he would have gone very far before finding somewhere to hide."

"That's true!" MacKenzie exclaimed. "Why, he could be near us right now."

"He might have hidden in one of these warehouses temporarily," the stout First Investigator said, "but he wouldn't be safe there, and he'd have to eat. So I think he would have looked for a motel or a rooming house not too far from here. He wouldn't have wanted to be out on the street for long."

"Then," Ndula said, "I suggest we split up and search for such a place in all three directions. We can look down any side streets as we go along."

Pete and Ndula went to the right, Jupiter and MacKenzie to the left, and Bob took the cross street alone. They agreed to meet again at the alley in no more than an hour.

Bob was the first one to return. He had gone all the way up the small cross street until it ended at a broad open field. He had found no motels or rooming houses or any other likely hiding places for a fugitive. It was already past lunchtime, and Bob paced hungrily by the alley while he waited for the others to come back.

Jupiter and MacKenzie were next.

"There is a small motel about five blocks away near the freeway," MacKenzie reported, "but they haven't had a boy staying there alone anytime this week. They recognized Jupiter only because his picture has been in the newspaper."

"It's mostly open fields and vacant lots in that direction, all the way to the freeway," Jupiter added.

Pete and Ndula finally returned. They had gone the farthest.

"All the way into town," Pete said. "We found a motel and two rooming houses, but none of them had a boy staying alone there."

"The rooming houses haven't had any transients in months," Ndula added.

"Ian was running with the kidnappers close behind," MacKenzie said slowly. "There would have been little chance to leave clues, and no hope that a message to us would ever be found. We are truly at a dead end now, boys."

"He's right, Jupe," Bob said.

"We do seem to be stumped for now," Jupiter admitted reluctantly.

"I think Adam and I had best return to our hotel and find out if Ian has called Los Angeles," MacKenzie decided. "He must know we are trying to find him, and that we've lost his trail. Perhaps he'll try to send another message through the trade mission."

"If he can," Ndula said grimly.

"And we'll return to Headquarters and consider further plans," Jupiter said stubbornly. "We're not far from the salvage yard here. Would you drop us off, Mac?"

"Hey, it's way past lunchtime," Pete protested. "I'm going home."

"Bob, you might as well go home and eat, too," Jupiter said. "I want to do some thinking anyway."

They returned to the big Cadillac. The Nandans dropped Jupiter off first at the salvage yard, little more than a mile away. Bob and Pete agreed to meet at Headquarters in an hour, and MacKenzie drove them to their homes.

But it was nearly two hours before Bob and Pete met with Jupiter again inside the hidden house trailer. They found their stout leader surrounded by street maps and papers covered with scrawled lists and notes.

"Any new ideas, First?" Pete asked at once.

"Yes, Second, I have a few ideas," Jupiter said, and then sighed unhappily, "but not many."

"MacKenzie and Ndula didn't call?" Bob asked. "Ian hasn't contacted the trade mission?"

"I called them, Records, and, no, Ian hasn't made any contact yet," Jupiter said.

"Jupe?" Pete said, frowning as he thought hard. "I've been thinking—maybe they've got him! Maybe those kidnappers came back and this time got the right kid! They must have seen the story in the newspapers about you and learned they'd made a mistake."

"Yes, I thought of that." Jupiter nodded. "It's possible that they have got him, but I don't think so. If they did, I'm certain they would have sent a message to Sir Roger, and so far they haven't. Besides, Pete, you saw someone watching us from that vacant lot across the street, and I've got a pretty good hunch it was the kidnappers."

"Ulp!" Pete swallowed hard. "You mean they're around somewhere right now?"

"I'm certain that they aren't far away, and that they're watching either us or MacKenzie and Ndula," Jupiter said. "We must be careful, but I think we're safe until we do find Ian."

"Fellows?" Bob said suddenly. "If Ian read that newspaper story about Jupe, wouldn't he have come out of hiding and gone to the police? I mean, when they saw him they'd know he was the real kid the kidnappers were after, and he'd be safe!"

"Wow, sure!" Pete exclaimed.

"I agree," Jupiter said. "Which means that Ian didn't see the story. He probably is hiding someplace where he hasn't had a chance to see a newspaper, and is too scared to come out. If only we could figure out where!"

"You said you had some ideas, Jupe?" Pete reminded him.

"Well, I thought about running an ad in the newspaper," Jupiter said. "Something coded so that only Ian could know it was for him, with a message to meet Mac-Kenzie and Ndula somewhere. But then I realized that if Ian couldn't see the newspaper, an ad wouldn't do much good."

"I'm afraid not, First," Bob agreed.

"Then, we could try a Ghost-to-Ghost Hookup," Jupiter went on, referring to the brilliant information-gathering technique he'd devised. When using it, the Investigators would each call five friends and ask them to pass a message on to five of their friends, and so on. "With all the kids in Rocky Beach, someone should be able to spot a strange boy with an accent."

"If he ever comes out of hiding," Bob pointed out.

"And if they don't mistake him for you," added Pete.

"That is a problem," Jupiter admitted, "so we won't consider the Ghost-to-Ghost until at least tomorrow. Meanwhile, there are two other things I've been thinking about. Ian must realize by now that anyone who's looking for him lost the trail at that alley four days ago. The last place any rescuers could be sure of is the Red Lion Ranch. So—"

"So he might try to go back there and find anyone looking for him!" Pete exclaimed.

"Exactly, Second. He'd probably sneak up and be wary, so I suggested that MacKenzie and Ndula stake out the Red Lion and watch for him. They're probably out there right now."

"What's the other thing you thought about?" Bob asked.

"Something I've sort of wondered about at the back of my mind all along," Jupiter said. "How did the kidnappers spot me in the first place, and mistake me for Ian?"

"Gee," Pete said, "I guess they saw you here in the yard."

"Why would they have come around the yard at all unless they already knew that a boy who looked like Ian was here?"

"They probably just spotted you in the street and followed you here," Bob decided.

"Sure," Pete agreed. "They thought they'd gotten lucky and found Ian."

"Perhaps," Jupiter said. "But I feel we're missing something important. Those men must have had something more to go on than accidentally seeing me in the street."

"What, Jupe?"

"I don't know."

After that the Three Investigators sat in silence. None of them had any new ideas of what to do, so Bob and Pete went home. Jupiter walked moodily across the street to his house to watch television before dinnertime. Then Uncle Titus asked him to help find an error in the salvage yard account books, and he was busy until Aunt Mathilda called them to the table.

Despite the frustrating day, Jupiter ate heartily. He held out his plate for seconds, and grinned.

"Your beef stew is the best, Aunt Mathilda."

"Hmmph," Aunt Mathilda snorted. "It boggles my mind how you can eat anything the way you've been raiding my refrigerator, young man."

"I haven't been raiding the refrigerator, Aunt Mathilda," Jupiter protested. "I told you that yesterday. Gosh, Pete even lost his—"

Jupiter stopped with his mouth open and his eyes wide. He gulped, and blinked at his aunt. She stared at him.

"Are you all right, Jupiter?" Uncle Titus asked.

"I . . . I'm fine, Uncle Titus! I've never been better!" He jumped up. "Can I leave for a minute?"

"Before dessert, young man?" Aunt Mathilda said.

"I'll have it in a minute."

He hurried into the living room and quickly dialed Bob's number.

"Records! Get Pete and come to Headquarters right away! And tell your parents you'll be staying with me all night!"

Jupiter hung up and went back to the table. He was so excited that he could eat only two pieces of Aunt Mathilda's best apple pie, and gulp down only one large glass of milk. Then he asked to be excused, and hurried out of the house toward the hidden headquarters trailer under its mounds of junk.

When Bob and Pete came scrambling up through the trap door from Tunnel Two fifteen minutes later, Jupiter was seated at the desk, grinning at them.

"What is it, First?" Bob wanted to know, out of breath from biking so hard from his house.

"Why are we going to stay all night?" Pete demanded.

"Because, fellows," Jupiter announced triumphantly, "I know where Ian Carew is hiding!"

13

Face to Face!

"Where, First?" Bob cried.

"How do you know?" Pete exclaimed.

"It's been in front of our noses all the time," Jupiter declared. "We've been blind, fellows! I knew we were missing something important. I was sure the kidnappers didn't just see me on a street and follow me to the yard."

"Why not, Jupe?" Pete demanded.

"Because if they had, they would have seen at once that I wasn't a runaway trying to hide! They would have seen me with friends, acting like someone who lived in Rocky Beach. They might even have heard me speak, and then they would never have made their mistake."

"But, Jupe," Bob said, "they *did* make the mistake!"

"Yes, they did," Jupiter said, "and that's the answer. They made the mistake because they saw me exactly where they expected to see Ian! Where they were looking for Ian!"

"Looking for him?" Bob gaped.

"Yes, Records. Somewhere not far from where Ian left that taxi. Someplace where food has been disappearing for the last few days!" Jupiter's eyes glowed. "Fellows, Ian's hiding right here in the salvage yard!"

"In . . . in the . . . yard?" Pete gaped.

"Only a mile from that alley where he vanished," Bob said in awe. "Rats didn't get your lunch, Pete, Ian did!"

"Precisely, Records," Jupiter said. "When Ian ran from that alley with the kidnappers close behind him, he must have reached the salvage yard. He must have decided that all the junk would make a good hiding place, and that my house would be a good place to steal food. The kidnappers followed him to the yard, or at least nearby, and kept on driving around until they saw me! They naturally assumed I was Ian, since I was right in the area where they expected him to be. So they went after me, and made their mistake!"

"Right here in the yard all the time?" Pete said, still unbelieving.

"I'm sure of it," Jupiter stated. "Now all we have to do is find him."

"Find him?" Pete frowned. "Let's just go out and yell!"

Jupiter shook his head. "No, I don't think that would work, Second. He doesn't know us, and he's probably only seen us from a distance. He must be well hidden, because if he'd seen MacKenzie or Ndula he would have come out. If we went out and yelled, or even searched, we'd probably only scare him into running away again. And it's hard to find anyone in all that junk, as we know."

"Gosh, Jupe," Pete protested, "doesn't he have to come out sometime? I mean, he can't hide here forever."

"No, he can't. When he feels it to be safe, he'll probably return to the Red Lion Ranch or call the Nandan Trade Mission in Los Angeles. In the meantime, he'll stay hidden."

"Then what do we do, Jupe?" Bob asked.

"I have a plan," Jupiter declared. "I suspect that Ian

ventures out only late at night when everything is quiet."

"That's why you wanted us to stay with you all night," Pete realized.

"Yes, Second."

"Do we set a trap, Jupe? Lie in wait?" Bob asked.

"That is my plan," Jupiter answered. "My guess is that Ian comes out only when he wants some food. He's a clever boy, so he's taken as little food as possible—just enough to make Aunt Mathilda think that someone in the family is raiding the refrigerator. That means he can't have a lot of food with him, and we can set a trap."

"With food, sure." Pete nodded.

"I'm certain he won't come out until the yard is deserted. So the first thing we'll do is go out in the yard and talk a lot, making sure Ian hears us wherever he is."

"Talk about what?"

"About a trip we're going to take tomorrow, and about the three lunches we're going to pack tonight and leave out on the back porch of my house so we can get an early start."

"I get it," Pete said. "Three lunches would last him a while, so he'll be really tempted."

Jupiter nodded. "He'll figure we'd blame the theft on tramps or something. Anyway, we'll leave the yard about ten o'clock, put some dummy lunches on the back porch, and then go upstairs to bed. At least, two of us will go to bed. The third will sneak back downstairs and hide just inside the kitchen where he can watch the porch. We'll take turns watching, two hours each, while the other two get some sleep.

"We'll all have our emergency signals. The one on watch will keep his turned off. When he spots Ian, he'll

activate the signal with the usual voice command—
'Help!' The signals in my bedroom will then start beeping, and the red lights on them will flash. The beeps will
be loud enough to wake the sleepers!"

"Then what?" asked Bob.

"The two in my bedroom will get up fast and go out
the front way. They'll circle around the house in both
directions. The one in the kitchen will give the others
about two minutes, and then he'll set up a yell and chal-
lenge Ian. When Ian runs, he'll have to head for the front
of the house, because that's the only way back to his
hiding place in the salvage yard. So he'll run into one of
us. That person will grab him and hold on until the other
two arrive."

"Then we can tell him who we are and about Mac-
Kenzie and Ndula, right, First?" Pete concluded.

Jupiter nodded. "Just don't make too much noise. My
aunt and uncle are sound sleepers, but a real ruckus will
wake them up. Now, I suggest we get our emergency signals from the workshop and busy ourselves in the yard
until ten o'clock."

The Investigators worked around the outdoor workshop, making a good deal of noise, and then took a noisy
stroll around the entire junkyard. They pretended to be
hunting for walking sticks to take on a hiking trip the
next day. Talking loudly, they discussed their trip and
the lunches they would get ready and leave on the porch
for a quick start. Shortly before ten, the boys switched
off the outdoor lights in the yard and went across the
street to Jupe's house.

Once inside they quickly made the three dummy
lunches, stuffing wadded-up newspaper into brown paper

bags, and put them out in the enclosed back porch. Then
the boys went upstairs to Jupiter's room. Bob drew the
first two-hour watch. He waited until Aunt Mathilda and
Uncle Titus came upstairs, then slipped back down to
the dark kitchen. Pete and Jupiter tucked their beepers
into their shirt pockets, so they'd be sure to hear them
when they went off, and went to sleep in their clothes.

At midnight Jupiter replaced Bob.

The lunches were untouched on the back porch. Out
in the night nothing moved except distant cars on the
freeway, and from time to time a solitary walker on the
street.

Pete took over at 2:00 A.M. He yawned, and thought
about raiding the refrigerator himself. By the time Bob
came to take over again at 4:00 A.M., he was discouraged.

"Maybe Jupe's wrong?" Pete whispered. "Or maybe
Ian's already left the yard? Or maybe we aren't fooling
him?"

"I'm sure Jupe's right," Bob whispered, and then added
uneasily, "but maybe Ian has gone somewhere else. This
isn't the only house on this street, though it's the closest."

At 5:30 A.M. a gray light began to tinge the eastern
sky, but the yard and house remained in darkness. Then
something moved just outside the back porch!

Bob jerked fully awake. He blinked and peered toward
the movement. A shadowy figure stood just outside the
porch door!

Bob activated his emergency signal, whispering softly
into it, "Help . . . help . . . help . . ."

Upstairs, the emergency signals began beeping strongly
and flashing their red lights. Jupiter leaped out of bed
and almost fell over. Quickly he shut off the beepers and
stood listening, holding his breath. But there was no

sound below. Still fully dressed, he shook Pete awake.

"Hurry!" Jupiter whispered.

They slipped down to the front door. Outside the house they separated and circled quickly to the back. Each found a bush to hide behind.

In the kitchen Bob checked his watch. The porch door was silently opening. The shadowy figure of a stout boy, shaped exactly like Jupiter, stood outlined by the faint light of early dawn. The figure moved forward and reached out to take the lunches.

"Stop!" Bob cried. "You! Ian Carew!"

With a faint cry, the boy whirled and raced out of the porch. He stumbled down the steps, fell headlong, leaped up, and ran on. He was looking back at Bob as he rounded the corner of the house. Jupiter leaped out on top of him.

"Oooofffff!" Jupiter grunted as they collided.

"Ahhhrrrrrrrr!" the fleeing boy raged.

The boy almost pulled away, but Bob and Pete ran up just in time to grab him. He struggled wildly with his three captors.

"We're friends, Ian!"

"Working for Sir Roger!"

"We're trying to help you! MacKenzie—!"

But the frantic boy went on struggling until they got him down. Pete sat on him while Jupiter briefly told their story.

"Gordon MacKenzie?" the boy said. "Mr. Ndula? They're really here?"

"Yes, Ian," Jupiter said. "You're safe now. Or you will be when we get you into our headquarters. Hurry, fellows!"

Jupe paused to scoop up his emergency signal, which

had fallen out of his shirt pocket in the melee, and stuffed the unit into his pants pocket. The Investigators dragged the hesitant boy up and hustled him across the dimly lit street and through Green Gate One. Then they guided him into Tunnel Two.

"Where . . . where are you taking me?" Ian asked.

"To our hidden trailer," Jupiter explained a: he crawled through the tunnel behind him. "Those men who want to kidnap you may be around somewhere outside."

Pete pushed up the trap door, and they all scrambled up into the dark trailer. Bob switched on the light. The boy's mouth dropped open and his eyes widened in amazement as he saw Jupiter.

"Why . . . why, you look just like me!"

14

A Startling Discovery

"No," Jupiter said, grinning, "*you* look just like *me!*"

Ian Carew grinned in return. "Since we are in your country, I suppose you're right."

"Especially," Pete said, "in those clothes."

Ian was wearing an old pair of Jupiter's pants, a plain white shirt that Jupiter had worn out months ago, and a torn pair of sneakers.

"I'm afraid my clothes were ruined during my efforts to evade capture," Ian explained, "and while crawling around through the junk on the first day of my sojourn here. I was forced to avail myself of these articles which I found in a rag box!"

"Oh, no!" Pete groaned. "They even sound alike! I don't think I can stand two identical Jupes!"

Everyone laughed.

"I'm sorry to create twins," Ian said, "but I must say I'm awfully glad you chaps found me. I was beginning to wonder if anyone ever would."

"I'm glad we found each other." Jupiter beamed at his double.

"It certainly is good not to be alone any longer," Ian said. "But, I say, I don't even know your names!"

"Your double there is Jupiter Jones, First Investigator,"

Bob said. "I'm Bob Andrews, Records and Research. And the tall, groaning one is Pete Crenshaw, Second Investigator."

"Investigators?" Ian wondered. "Really?"

"Our card, sir!" Jupiter intoned, and handed Ian one of their Three Investigators cards.

"How marvelous!" Ian cried enviously. "You Americans do such exciting things. You're really detectives?"

"Hired by Mr. Ndula and Mr. MacKenzie to help find you," Bob said. "After your pursuers had mistaken Jupe for you and kidnapped him!"

"They actually kidnapped you, Jupiter?" Ian exclaimed.

Jupiter explained the rest of their adventures since they had become involved in the case. Ian listened intently.

"So you deduced what I meant by Djanga's place," the fugitive boy said, "and found the taxi I drew at the Red Lion?"

"And guessed you were here in the salvage yard," Pete added proudly.

"Jolly good work," Ian enthused. "But now what, eh? Shall we get in touch with MacKenzie and Ndula so they can tell my father that I'm safe?"

"Sure," Pete agreed. "We can take Ian right over to the Miramar Hotel."

"Is that a good idea?" Bob said slowly. "I mean, those kidnappers could be watching outside the yard, or watching MacKenzie and Ndula at the Miramar."

"Do you really think so?" Ian cried, alarmed.

"Bob's right," Jupiter decided. "It's possible. As Ndula and MacKenzie said, those extremists won't give up

easily. I'm sure we're safe in the yard, and there's no
sense in taking any unnecessary chances. Better to call
MacKenzie and Ndula, and have them come over here."

"I'll call," Bob said.

As he dialed the number of the Miramar Hotel, Ian
looked curiously around the trailer. He saw the office
with its desk and file cabinet, the tiny laboratory that
also served as a darkroom, and the intriguing detective
equipment that lay all around.

"You chaps are quite cozy in here, aren't you? Odd
that I never noticed this trailer from outside."

"It's not odd at all," Pete said. "You can't see a trace of
it from outside. We completely covered it with junk, and
not even Jupe's aunt and uncle remember that it's here!"

"Wonderful!" Ian cried.

Bob hung up the phone. "No answer from the Nandans'
room, First. The clerk doesn't know where they are, so
I said we'd call back. I didn't want to leave a message—
it could be spotted."

"Good thinking, Records," Jupiter said. "They're probably watching the Red Lion, as I suggested. One of them
should return to the Miramar soon." He turned to Ian.
"Incidentally, what had you planned to do if we hadn't
found you, Ian?"

"When I felt it to be safe, I was going to return to the
Red Lion and see if anyone had followed me that far."

"Just as I thought," Jupiter said a little smugly.

"You weren't going to contact the trade mission?" Bob
asked.

"Only as a last resort. When those kidnappers appeared
at the Red Lion, I realized they had some way of finding
out about messages sent through the mission—and that

they knew enough about me to decode any secret message."

Jupiter reached into a desk drawer and took out the tiny ivory and gold tusk the Investigators had found in the box canyon.

"Have you ever seen this before, Ian?"

Ian studied it. "Well, it's certainly made in Nanda, and there *is* something familiar about it. I think I have seen it before, but I can't remember where."

"Bob," Pete urged, "try the Miramar again."

While Bob went to the phone, Ian took a closer look at the Investigators' equipment. He saw a periscope that could rise through the trailer's roof, a loudspeaker for the telephone, walkie-talkies, a microscope, even a camera for closed-circuit television.

"Where did you get so much equipment, chaps?" he asked.

"We made most of it ourselves," Pete said. "Or Jupe did. Using parts and broken sets that arrived in the junkyard.

"We've got a workshop outside," Jupiter added.

"Workshop? Why, I've got one back home, too!"

"You've been in ours," Jupiter said. "We came through it to get in here, though you couldn't see it in the dark. But you were in the workshop when you swiped Pete's lunch the other day!"

"I'm afraid I didn't notice at the time," Ian said, laughing. "Can I see it now? While we're waiting?"

Bob looked up from the telephone. "They think Ndula just returned. He's on his way up to the room. I'll hold on."

"We'll be in the workshop," Pete said.

Pete, Jupiter, and Ian went down through the trap door and crawled out into the sheltered workshop. The dawn was full and bright now, with the sun already up in the east. Ian glanced around nervously.

"I say, are we safe here?"

"Oh, yes," Jupiter assured him. "No one can see over the junkyard fence, and the piles of junk around this workshop keep it private from the rest of the yard. We'd see anyone who came close."

Ian nodded cheerfully. He began to study all the tools on the long workbench and along the sides of the workshop area. Jupiter pointed out the band saw, the lathe, and the printing press. Ian eagerly studied everything.

"I must say, it's very well equipped," he exclaimed with admiration.

Bob came crawling out of Tunnel Two.

"I talked to Ndula!" he said excitedly. "He's going to pick up MacKenzie and they'll drive over right away."

"In a way I wish they wouldn't," Ian said. "I'd like to stay and inspect your headquarters all day." He bent and reached down to the shelf under the workbench. "I say, chaps, what is this for?"

He held out a small black boxlike object about the size of a folder of safety matches.

"That?" Pete explained. "That's a . . . that's a . . . Jupe, what *is* that?"

Bob took the little box. "Why, it's a . . . it's a—"

"Fellows!" Jupiter stared at the small object. "That's not anything of ours! That's a bug!"

"Bug?" Ian said. "But isn't a bug an insect?"

"A listening device!" Jupiter cried. "A tiny microphone! Someone is listening to us! Hurry, we must get—"

The voice spoke from outside the workshop—a familiar voice to all of them!

"No hurry, boys. You're not going anywhere!"

The stocky kidnapper with the curly brown hair stepped into the workshop. The tall, dark one walked behind him.

They both held pistols aimed straight at the boys!

15

A Problem for the Enemy!

"Well, here we all are," the stocky kidnapper said with a nasty smile.

"It looks like we have our boy, Walt," the tall one said.

"It does look that way, doesn't it, Fred?"

"We should thank these smart lads, eh?" Fred said. "This time they did us a favor! Made it nice and easy for us."

"We do thank them, Fred." Walt laughed.

The two Nandan extremists seemed to be enjoying their banter, and seemed to be in no hurry. If Mac-Kenzie and Ndula arrived soon . . . !

"You won't get away with this!" Bob warned hotly.

"It won't do you any good with Sir Roger anyway!" Pete added fiercely.

"But we *will* get away with it, my boy," Walt said blandly. "And we shall see about Sir Roger, eh?"

The stocky kidnapper smiled, and looked first at Ian and then at Jupiter. The other man was watching Jupiter and Ian, too. Bob and Pete saw a sudden gleam in Jupiter's eyes.

"You were quite clever, young Jones," Walt said, "not revealing who you were or letting us know we had the wrong boy. Jolly good thing we slipped back here after abandoning the helicopter, eh? We read the newspaper and saw our error. We guessed that Master Carew was still in this area, so while the authorities were searching the state for us, we watched this yard."

"We spotted MacKenzie and that Ndula savage," Fred added with a grin. "When you boys joined them, we knew you'd lead us to Ian sooner or later. It was child's play to mingle with all the customers who come into this junkyard. You were all so involved in your attempt to locate Ian that you never noticed us."

"We saw you!" Pete raged.

"Across the street? Yes, that was a near thing," Walt agreed. "But no harm done. We saw you later in this workshop and quite easily planted the microphone while you were away."

The two kidnappers were standing with their backs to a massive mound of junk, which was close behind them. Bob glanced quickly toward Jupiter. The boys had the mound of junk booby-trapped so that it could be pulled down on an enemy in just such an emergency. Jupiter shook his head briefly—they would not take such a chance with men holding guns. But Jupiter's eyes were still gleaming. What was Jupe planning?

"Every policeman in the state is after you!" Pete declared, stalling for time.

"They'll find you," Bob added.

"Ah, but we have our hostage, don't we?" Walt said.

"No one will touch us," Fred said mockingly.

"So, Ian, time to go," Walt announced.

"You don't want anyone hurt," Fred cautioned him.

Ian stepped forward. "No, I'll go with you chaps."

Jupiter stepped out beside Ian. "No, I'll go with you chaps."

"I say, Jupiter," Ian said. "You mustn't risk yourself."

"I say, Jupiter," Jupiter echoed him exactly. "You mustn't risk yourself." He suddenly added, "We really can't fool these fellows, Jupiter. They know I'm really Ian."

Jupiter was using a British accent! An accent the same as Ian's!

"Jupiter!" Ian protested. "We *really* mustn't try to fool them. They're sure to know that I am Ian."

The two kidnappers stood glaring at both boys, all their smiles and banter gone. It was suddenly obvious that they *didn't* know which boy was which! Bob realized what the gleam in Jupiter's eyes had meant—Jupiter had realized that the kidnappers weren't sure who was who. The doubles looked alike, were dressed alike, and now—thanks to Jupe—sounded alike!

"All right," Walt said menacingly, "this trick has gone far enough. I want the real Ian Carew to speak out now!"

"It could get bad for one of you," Fred warned.

"Please, Jupiter," Ian said. "I must go with them!"

"Stop it, Jupiter," Jupiter said. "They know I am Ian now. You are far too anxious to go with them!"

The kidnappers looked furiously at the two boys.

"It's the second one, in the print shirt," Fred decided. "He's right, that first kid is too anxious to go! He's fooling us."

"But the real Ian Carew *would* try to save his friends by cooperating," Walt said. "Search them!"

Pistol in hand, Fred advanced on both boys.

"Try their clothes," Walt ordered. "Laundry marks!"

Fred looked inside Jupiter's shirt collar in the back. "That did it, Walt! Here it is: Jones 1127!"

Jupiter shrugged. "I tore my clothes running from you.

I got these here in the salvage yard. Try his shirt."

Fred looked inside Ian's shirt collar. He swore an oath. "Jones 1127! It's no good!"

Ian nodded. "Yes, I did ruin my clothes, and found a shirt and pants in Jupiter's salvage yard. And I have nothing at all in my pockets, which proves I am Ian!"

"Then that makes two Ians, Jupiter," Jupiter said. "I'm afraid that my pockets are also quite empty since these are not my clothes."

Bob and Pete gaped. Of course! Jupiter had slept in his clothes the night before, so had removed everything from his pockets.

"However, gentlemen," Jupiter went on in his British accent, "Jupiter there does have something in his shirt pocket, and it will prove he is Jupiter Jones!"

Fred reached quickly into Ian's shirt pocket. He brought out the small listening device, and turned to his partner.

"It's our bug! This is the Jones boy's workshop, so I guess he would be the one who'd keep the bug!"

"Idiot!" Walt fumed. "We heard Ian Carew find the bug, and then they passed it all around! Who knows who kept it? And don't take their word for what they've got on them—search!"

Red-faced, Fred turned back angrily to the boys and bumped hard into Jupiter, who had been standing close behind him. Jupiter had to grab the kidnapper's jacket to keep from falling. Swearing, Fred disentangled himself.

"Keep your hands off, boy! And stand right there."

The tall kidnapper searched him thoroughly, then turned and searched Ian.

"Nothing on either of them. It's hopeless, Walt."

Jupiter was grinning, and, suddenly, so was Ian.

"Let's end this now," Walt said. "Ian Carew's father has a chauffeur. A soldier. What's his name and rank? One of you can prove he's Ian, and we'll let Jones go."

Bob and Pete froze. There was no way Jupiter could know the answer. Ian could prove who he was.

"All right," Ian said. "You've got me. I'm Jupiter Jones!"

Bob and Pete showed no expression, but in their minds they cheered. Ian had caught on to Jupe's game and was playing it, too!

"Yes, I admit it," Jupiter said. "I'm Jupiter Jones."

The pair of kidnappers glared in black anger. Walt turned to Bob and Pete.

"Perhaps you two have enough sense to stop your friend from being a fool. Tell us which one he is."

"Him!" Pete pointed at Ian.

"Him!" Bob pointed at Jupiter.

Walt nodded slowly. "Very well, then there's only one thing left to do."

He started to walk toward the two almost identical boys.

16

A Dangerous Action

Adam Ndula picked up Gordon MacKenzie at the Red Lion Ranch, and then drove the big Cadillac through the now sunny morning to the salvage yard. They hurried in through the main gate. None of the boys was there to meet them. They looked all around the silent yard, deserted still in the early morning.

"Ian!" MacKenzie called out. "Jupiter?"

"Bob said they had Ian in their hidden headquarters, wherever that is," Ndula said, and called out, "Jupiter Jones!"

"Ian! Jupiter!"

"Stars and stripes, what a racket!" Aunt Mathilda appeared around the corner of the yard office. "Do you know what time of the morning it is, you howling coyotes!"

"Sorry, ma'am," MacKenzie said quickly, "but we're looking for the boys. Have you seen Jupiter?"

"Oh, it's you two. Grown men acting like banshees!"

"Can you tell us where your nephew is?" Ndula asked.

"No, I can't," Aunt Mathilda snapped. "He and his pals sneaked out early to go heaven knows where."

"But they asked us to meet them here," Ndula said.

"Then they're probably skulking around the yard. Try

their workshop. Straight to your left to that big mound of salvage, then follow—"

"Thank you," interrupted MacKenzie, "but I believe we've been there before."

The two Nandans hurried across the yard to the outdoor workshop. They found it deserted.

"They're not here!" MacKenzie exclaimed.

"What's that?" Ndula said, listening.

A low thumping seemed to come from somewhere nearby. A metallic thumping and clanging, and a muffled sound like grunts.

"It's over there!" Ndula cried. "That large pipe!"

They ran to the opening of the big pipe and peered in. Bob and Pete lay bound and stuffed into the pipe! The two Nandans reached in and hauled them out, quickly removing their bonds and the gags in their mouths.

"The kidnappers!" Pete wailed.

"They took them!" Bob said despairingly.

"Them?" MacKenzie repeated. "You mean, Ian and Jupiter? The kidnappers took them? When?"

"Not five minutes ago." Pete groaned. "Maybe less! They couldn't tell which kid was which, and Ian and Jupe wouldn't tell them—so the men took both of them!"

"Where are they taking them?" Ndula asked.

"We don't know!"

"What kind of car? Did you get the license number?"

"We never even saw their car!"

"They can't be far yet," MacKenzie said. "The police can—"

"Peter?" Ndula stared. "Your chest, it looks like it's on fire! There's a flashing red light!"

"It's your emergency signal, Second!" Bob cried. "It

must be Jupe! Quick, turn it on and read the directional dial!"

Pete pulled the small signal from his shirt pocket. The red light was flashing off and on irregularly. As Pete turned the instrument on, it began to beep loudly, and the arrow on the dial pointed directly toward the center of Rocky Beach.

"Listen how loud it is!" Pete exclaimed. "That means they haven't gone far yet!"

"And they're heading *into* town, not away," Bob said. "Mac, hurry! We'll go after them! There may still be time!"

The two Nandans and the boys ran out of the yard to the big black Cadillac. Pete bent over the signal dial. The beeps were loud and clear.

"That way!" Pete pointed. "Straight toward town!"

Ndula drove off swiftly. MacKenzie looked at the signal.

"Just what is that instrument? How does it work?"

"It's a directional signal and emergency alarm," Bob explained as the beeping grew even louder. "It's both a sender and a receiver. Right now this unit is receiving from Jupe's signal. That's why it's beeping. The beeps get louder and faster as you get closer to another unit, and the arrow on the dial shows which direction the signal is coming from. The unit also works as an emergency alarm—the red light flashes on voice command. My signal is flashing because Jupe is saying—"

"Don't say it!" yelled Pete. "You'll set off Jupe's signal!"

Bob gulped. "Right. Jupe is managing to say h-e-l-p near his signal, so this one is now flashing."

"Turn right, Adam!" Pete suddenly instructed. "The

beeps are getting louder all the time. I think the kid-nappers must have stopped!"

MacKenzie frowned. "Each unit is both a sender and receiver, Bob? And Jupiter is operating one in the car with those kidnappers? What happens if we accidentally set off his signal?"

"I'm sure he has his beeper turned off," Bob explained, "so the men won't hear it. And he's probably got the signal hidden in a pocket so they won't spot the red light if it starts flashing."

"I hope it's well hidden," MacKenzie said slowly, "be-cause he's taking a very dangerous action. If those men catch him using the signal, they'll know at once which boy is Jupiter!"

Bob paled. "Hurry, Adam!"

The rented blue Lincoln of the kidnappers had pulled into a self-service gas station. Jupiter and Ian sat in the back seat with Walt while Fred filled the gas tank. No one came near the sleek car.

"It'll go easier on both of you if you tell us which of you is Ian Carew," Walt said.

"Help will come," Jupiter said. "I know we'll get help."

"Yes," Ian agreed, "our friends will send help."

"Help might just be too late," Walt snarled. "If Jones gets out of this car right now, we'll let him go. He can just walk away. But if we don't identify him till later—well, we may have to dispose of him!"

"I don't believe you," Ian said.

"Neither do I," Jupiter said. "Help is going to come."

"Don't be stupid, Jones," Walt said, looking from one of them to the other. "This isn't your affair. If you're worried about Ian, we won't hurt him. We need him for important matters. We want him very safe."

"Until he can't be of any more help to you," Jupiter said.

"If we have to take both of you," Walt snarled again, "who knows what could happen to Jones, eh?"

The boys paled, but neither of them spoke. Fred got back into the driver's seat.

"Okay, Walt, we gave them their chance. Now we'll settle the problem our way. These boys aren't as clever as they think they are!"

Ndula drove the Cadillac as fast as he dared through the streets of Rocky Beach. Pete sat beside him watching the signal dial. Bob and MacKenzie leaned forward to watch from the back seat. The beeping suddenly began to slow and grow softer!

"Turn right!" Pete cried, as he saw the arrow on the dial swing sharply toward the ocean.

Ndula turned at the next street. It was a broad main street that led to the harbor, and it was crowded now with morning rush-hour traffic. The beeps slowed further, and began to grow weaker and weaker!

"They've turned south again!" Pete cried.

"Pete!" Bob said. "They must have gone onto the freeway! The arrow is pointing half south and half east! Toward Los Angeles."

"I . . . I think you're right, Records," Pete groaned.

"How far ahead is the freeway?" MacKenzie asked.

"At least a mile," Bob said.

Ndula shook his head. "I can't go fast in this traffic."

"On the freeway they can go four times as fast as we

can," MacKenzie said wearily. "What's the range of your signals, boys?"

"Only about three miles," answered Bob.

Helpless as the Cadillac moved slowly ahead on the crowded street, they watched the arrow begin to swing feebly, and listened to the beeps slowly fade away. Then the arrow slipped idly to dead center, the beeps stopped, and the red light went out.

"They're gone, boys," MacKenzie said. "We could never catch them now on the freeway, and we don't even know what their car looks like. It's time to go to the police."

In the back seat of the kidnappers' Lincoln, Ian and Jupiter huddled close together. Walt sat in the other corner, his gun in his lap and his eyes closed.

"You must tell them, Jupiter," Ian whispered into Jupe's ear. "They'll let you go."

"No," Jupiter whispered back. "They won't let me go. I'm safe while they don't know which of us is which. They won't harm Ian Carew, at least not yet. But they don't need Jupiter Jones, and I know too much about them."

Walt opened one eye. "Shut up, you two! We gave you your chance to talk. Now it won't be long before we can get rid of one of you!"

With a deadly laugh the kidnapper closed his eye again, and the Lincoln raced on through the sunny morning toward its unknown destination.

17

Pete Makes an Accusation

Pete, Bob, and the two Nandans waited on the long bench at police headquarters. Uncle Titus and Aunt Mathilda were with them. After the boys and the Nandans had told their story, the fiery Aunt Mathilda was unusually calm.

"This other boy, Ian Carew, is important to your country, Mr. Ndula?" she asked. "To its independence and future?"

"Yes, Mrs. Jones," Ndula said. "Very important. His father is our main hope for independence without civil war, for majority rule and a peaceful future. These kidnappers plan, by threatening Ian, to force Sir Roger to do what they want. So we must rescue Ian."

"And Jupiter and his friends were helping you find Ian when the kidnappers captured Jupiter?"

"I'm afraid so," MacKenzie said.

"Then the boys did what they should have," Aunt Mathilda announced. "I'm glad they tried to help you. Now we must get both boys back safely."

Chief Reynolds joined them, his face grim and serious.

"I've sent out the alarm to the Los Angeles police," the chief reported, "but I don't know what they can do. We have no description of the car, and no license number. All they can do is distribute the descriptions of the kidnappers to their patrol cars, and—"

"Again?" Aunt Mathilda said with a snort. "Seems to me you did that once before and got nowhere. They came back right under your noses!"

"Kidnappers don't usually return to the same area, Mrs. Jones. We had no reason to think they would do that."

"Yes, you did," Aunt Mathilda snapped. "Jupiter told you they weren't ordinary kidnappers! You should have listened."

"I suppose you're right, Mrs. Jones," Chief Reynolds admitted. "In any case, the Los Angeles police will have all their men looking for the kidnappers and the two boys. Not that they'll be able to move right away if they spot them."

"And why not, Chief?" Uncle Titus demanded.

"Because the kidnappers have Jupiter and Ian as hostages, Mr. Jones, and they're armed. From what MacKenzie and Ndula tell us, these men are more like soldiers than common criminals, and they are quite willing to sacrifice themselves to achieve their aims," the chief explained. "No, our only real hope is to track them somehow, and take them by surprise when they least expect it."

"But the boys are in great danger!" Uncle Titus cried.

"No," MacKenzie said. "I don't think they are in any immediate danger, Mr. Jones. The kidnappers must keep Ian safe or he'll be no use to them against Sir Roger, and I don't believe they will harm Jupiter. This is a political action, not a kidnapping for ransom, and they wouldn't want to anger the American government unnecessarily. Of course, if they reach Nanda things could become different."

"Then we'll make sure they don't get back to Nanda,"

Chief Reynolds said. "If we only had a hint of why they're going south to Los Angeles when they went north last time."

"They certainly have an escape route planned," Ndula said.

"For them and Ian!" Bob said suddenly. "But they've got two boys, and don't know which one is Ian. That's a problem they hadn't counted on, and it could have made them change plans!" Bob turned quickly to Mac-Kenzie and Ndula. "Is there some way they could identify Ian in Los Angeles?"

"Not that I know of, Bob," MacKenzie said.

"In Nanda," Ndula said, "but not in Los Angeles."

Pete thought. "Isn't there anyone at the Nandan Trade Mission who knows Ian? I mean, maybe a family friend?"

MacKenzie and Ndula looked at each other in surprise, as if they had never thought of the idea and wondered why.

"John Kearney?" Ndula suggested.

"He's a very old friend of Sir Roger's," MacKenzie said. "There's no way the boys could fool him. Only how would—"

"Who is this Kearney?" Chief Reynolds asked.

"The chief of our trade mission in Los Angeles," Mac-Kenzie explained. "But John Kearney would never help those extremists."

"Perhaps not," the chief conceded, "but Bob's right. They have a major problem they didn't expect, and they must solve it before they can continue with any escape plan. If they know that Kearney can identify Ian, they might very well try to trick him or startle him into revealing Ian. He should be warned at once."

"I'd better call him, then," MacKenzie said. "Those kidnappers have some way of learning what happens at the mission. Maybe we can trap them if they don't know that the police are aware of Kearney."

"Call him then," Chief Reynolds said. "Use my phone."

The others all waited impatiently while MacKenzie went to make the call. Aunt Mathilda paced nervously.

"What do you think the kidnappers will do if they can't find out which boy is Ian?" she asked Ndula.

"Then, I fear they will have to try to take both boys to Nanda," Ndula said.

"To Africa?" Aunt Mathilda cried. "Those villains!"

MacKenzie returned. "Kearney isn't at the mission office. He's supposed to be attending a series of meetings and exhibits in the Hollywood area on folk arts and handicrafts. His office doesn't know exactly where they all are. I didn't say anything about why I was calling. I think we should go to Los Angeles immediately."

"Yes!" Ndula exclaimed. "If the kidnappers do intend to see Kearney, and haven't yet, they'll have to go to the mission and we can trap them!"

"I'll radio the Los Angeles police to stake out the mission in case your man returns before we get there," the chief said. "They can warn him, and watch for the kidnappers."

Jupiter and Ian sat in the pitch dark of a small, windowless room. They had been alone for some hours since the kidnappers had hustled them out of the big Lincoln and into a small house high on a hill amid lush vegetation. Although their eyes had become accustomed to the darkness in the small room, they couldn't really see anything.

"Where are we, Jupiter?" Ian asked.

"I think somewhere in the Hollywood Hills," Jupiter said, "in somebody's storeroom or wine cellar." He had caught a brief glimpse of the room when the kidnappers shut them into it. He and Ian were securely tied up, so they couldn't search for a way out, but Jupe was fairly sure there was none.

"What do you think they're going to do with us?"

"They undoubtedly have some plan to slip you out of the country and back to Nanda, but why we are waiting here I don't know. Unless—"

"Unless what, Jupiter?" Ian said.

"Unless they are waiting for someone who can identify you positively," Jupiter said quietly.

"Yes, that's what I think too," Ian said, "and then they won't need *both* of us anymore. I wonder what they'll do to you."

"I wonder, too," Jupe said unhappily.

In the hot noon sun, Chief Reynolds turned his police car into the parking lot of an office building on Wilshire Boulevard. Ndula parked the big black Cadillac beside it. A Los Angeles police officer hurried up as the chief got out of his car.

"Mr. Kearney hasn't returned, Chief, and no suspicious parties have gone up to the trade mission. We have a man staked out up there."

"The kidnappers aren't near here, Chief," Pete added, staring at his emergency signal. "I'm getting no reading on my signal."

"Perhaps they've heard from Kearney upstairs," Ndula said.

"We'll find out," MacKenzie said, "but I think the chief should remain down here and not reveal that the police are watching."

The boys and the two Nandans went into the building and took the elevator up to the trade mission offices on the third floor. The receptionist greeted MacKenzie and Ndula, but then shook her head. She had not heard from Mr. Kearney.

"Both he and his assistant, Miss Lessing, are spending the day at those folk-art meetings," she explained. "Miss Lessing did say something about not staying out all day. If she comes back to the office early, perhaps she'll be able to tell you exactly where Mr. Kearney is. I do wish she would return. There have been calls for her and Mr. Kearney all morning, and I can't handle them."

The receptionist looked as if she was about to launch into a full list of her grievances, but fortunately the phone on her desk rang. She turned to answer it, and the visitors escaped out the door.

"There's the leak in the trade mission!" exclaimed Pete. "I'll bet she'd tell you anything about everything if you hung around her desk long enough!"

"Perhaps," said MacKenzie, laughing. "She does like to chat. But she can't tell us the one thing we want to know—where Kearney is."

"Which means she can't tell the kidnappers where he is, either," pointed out Ndula.

"Now what do we do?" asked Bob as they descended in the elevator.

"Wait and hope that someone shows up at the mission —the kidnappers, Miss Lessing, or Kearney," answered

MacKenzie. "I can't think of anything else."

The two Investigators, the Nandans, and some police-men spent several hot, frustrating hours in the parking lot. They kept an eye on Pete's emergency signal, but it never lit up.

"This is terrible!" groaned Pete. The Second Investi-gator had been getting more and more anxious. "Some-thing awful could have happened to Jupe and Ian by now. How do we know that the kidnappers haven't found somebody else to identify Ian?"

"We don't," said Ndula grimly. "But the trade mission is the only link to the kidnappers that we can think of, so we'll stay here."

Finally, in the middle of the afternoon, the plain-clothesman who was upstairs watching the mission called Chief Reynolds on his walkie-talkie.

"A dark-haired woman just walked in as if she be-longed here. Is that anybody you're looking for?"

"Miss Lessing!" exclaimed MacKenzie. "Maybe it's her! Everybody upstairs again!"

The receptionist looked up with a smile when Pete, Bob, and the Nandans entered the trade mission for the second time.

"Hello, again. There's been no word from Mr. Kearney, but Miss Lessing is back. Do you want to see her? She's in Mr. Kearney's office."

As they reached Mr. Kearney's private office in the far corner, Pete suddenly stopped and listened.

"What is it, Second?" Bob asked.

"I thought I heard people talking in the office. Maybe Miss Lessing is busy with someone."

Ndula listened. "I hear nothing, Pete."

"No," Pete said slowly, "I guess I was wrong."

They knocked, and went in. Miss Lessing stood beside Mr. Kearney's desk examining some papers. The tall, dark-haired woman wore a green blouse and the same gray slacks she had worn when she visited MacKenzie and Ndula at the hotel in Rocky Beach. Her eyes brightened when she saw them.

"Have you found Ian?"

"Found him," MacKenzie said bitterly, "and lost him."

"Lost?" Miss Lessing slowly picked up an earring from the desk and put it on.

"Have you been with Mr. Kearney all day, Miss Lessing?" Ndula asked.

She nodded.

"Did anyone ask him about Ian?"

"No." She shook her head. "No one. Why?"

"The kidnappers have him," MacKenzie explained, "and we think they're in Los Angeles looking for Kearney to—"

"Yes, of course!" Miss Lessing cried. "Mr. Kearney could identify Ian at once. They couldn't fool him. You must warn him immediately."

"Where can we reach him?" asked MacKenzie.

Miss Lessing looked at her watch. "By now he has to be at one of two places: the Handicraft Importers Guild or The Arts of Africa. Those are his two remaining appointments, and he must keep them both before five o'clock."

"That gives us an hour and a half to reach both places," Ndula calculated. "We can split up."

"Let's hurry," Bob cried.

Miss Lessing wrote out the addresses of the two places,

and the four visitors hurried out to the elevator. The moment the elevator doors closed, Pete turned to the other three.

"Mac, Adam, Bob! She's lying! She's sending us off on a wild goose chase!"

18

An Unexpected Foe

"What do you mean, Pete?" Bob cried.

"How can you know that?" Ndula snapped.

"You must be mistaken, Pete," MacKenzie said. "I've worked with Anna Lessing for years!"

"No, I'm not mistaken," Pete insisted. "She said that Mr. Kearney could identify Ian at once. She said they couldn't fool him."

MacKenzie was puzzled. "But that's all true. We told you that ourselves."

"Yeah," Pete agreed, "but we never told Miss Lessing that there was any problem about *identifying* Ian! We never said that the kidnappers had *two* boys!" He looked at the two Nandans and Bob. "So how did she know that the kidnappers were being fooled and needed to identify Ian?"

No one said anything. The elevator came to a stop at the ground floor, and they all got out. Ndula finally spoke.

"He's right," admitted the black Nandan. "We said only that the kidnappers had Ian and were probably in Los Angeles. In our phone calls to the trade mission, neither Gordon nor Chief Reynolds ever said anything about *two* boys."

MacKenzie nodded. "Outside of Rocky Beach, only the Los Angeles police know there are two boys, and they haven't spoken to anyone at the trade mission."

"The police *and* the kidnappers know there are two boys," Pete said. "And that means that Miss Lessing must have met the kidnappers here in Los Angeles today!"

"But," Ndula objected, "she was busy in meetings with Mr. Kearney all day."

"That's what *she* says," replied Pete.

"Mr. Kearney could verify her account," said Mac-Kenzie. "I doubt that she'd lie about her movements."

"Wait!" Bob cried. "Pete thought he heard someone talking in Mr. Kearney's office before we went in. We thought he was mistaken because Miss Lessing was alone in the office. But she picked up her earring from the desk and put it back on. I remember Jupe pointing out that women often take off an earring to talk on the phone! Maybe she was talking on the telephone to the kidnappers! Remember, the receptionist said Miss Lessing was getting a lot of calls. I'll bet the kidnappers have been trying to reach her all day!"

"Mac," Pete exclaimed, "you said you'd worked with her for years. Does that mean she worked with Sir Roger, too? Does she know Ian well enough to identify him positively?"

"I'm not sure." MacKenzie frowned. "She *has* been on Sir Roger's staff for years, but she's not a family friend, as Kearney is. Still, she could know something about Ian that would prove which boy he is. By George, she could easily have intercepted Ian's first message, too."

They rushed into the parking lot to share their deductions with Chief Reynolds.

"The extremists' contact in the trade mission!" Ndula

fumed. "We'll confront her! Make her tell us—"

"No," Chief Reynolds stopped him. "If she's in league with the extremists, she won't tell us anything. But she went to the trouble of sending you on a wild goose chase, which probably means she intends to join her confederates. She'll lead us to them!"

"After she thinks we've all gone to find Mr. Kearney," Pete said.

"Yes. I'll ask the Los Angeles police to remain here and watch for Kearney," the chief decided. "Then we'll all drive off in my car so she can see us leave. Once out of sight, we'll double back, and transfer to the Cadillac, and follow her. I doubt that she'll pay attention to a Cadillac behind her after she's seen us leave in a police car."

They did as the chief instructed. Fifteen minutes later, when Anna Lessing came out of the building alone and drove off in her red Pontiac, the black Cadillac followed her at a careful distance.

In the dark room in the house on the hill, Jupiter and Ian sat silently against the wall. They had been there for hours and hours.

"Your friends won't find us," Ian said. "Not now."

"They will! I know they will!" Jupiter said fiercely.

The lights suddenly went on, momentarily blinding the boys. Then they saw the two kidnappers in the small room. The stocky one, Walt, stepped up to Jupiter and ripped open his shirt. He turned quickly to Ian, and ripped his shirt.

"Well," he said, "the game's over, eh?"

Jupiter looked at Ian. Low on his stomach was a small, crooked scar. Jupiter had no scar.

"Next stop, Nanda," the kidnapper named Fred said, and laughed.

The red Pontiac turned into the driveway of a small house on the side of a steep hill in the Hollywood Hills. It stopped, and Anna Lessing ran quickly up some stairs into the house. The Cadillac following her parked quietly at the curb two houses away. Pete bent over his emergency signal.

"Nothing," he said, disappointed. "Unless the kidnappers found Jupe's signal and turned it off, they aren't around here."

"Could we be wrong, boys?" Ndula said.

"No, I'm convinced she's in with them!" Pete insisted.

"So am I," MacKenzie said. "Let's go and see what's in that house."

They left the big car and walked quickly and silently up to the small house. It was surrounded by a jungle of tall trees, vines, and bushes. They listened at the front door, but heard nothing inside except the click of Anna Lessing's heels on the wooden floor. MacKenzie rang the doorbell. Anna Lessing's jaw dropped when she opened the door.

"What the devil are you doing here!" she snapped, and then smiled uneasily. She stepped back and waved the group into a sparsely furnished living room. "Did you find Mr. Kearney? Have those kidnappers approached him?"

"We didn't look for him," Ndula said.

"We don't think they're looking for Kearney," MacKenzie added.

"We must warn you that you have the right to remain

silent," Chief Reynolds said, "but if you speak, anything you say may be used against you in a court of law."

"Where are they?" Pete cried. "Ian and Jupiter!"

"We know you've been talking to the kidnappers," Bob said angrily. "Where are they? What have they done with Jupiter and Ian?"

Anna Lessing stared at them all, and spread out her hands in protest.

"I don't know what you're talking about. Who is this Jupiter? I don't know any Jupiter. Why would I know where Ian is? Didn't you find Kearney?"

"You know who Jupiter Jones is," MacKenzie said. "And you know exactly what's happened to Ian because you're an accomplice of those kidnappers!"

"Accomplice?" She gaped at him. "Me? You mean you think I would harm Ian Carew? Me? I've been a friend of the Carews for years!"

"I think you're lying, Miss Lessing," Ndula said quietly. "Chief, maybe you'd better have a good look around."

"If you have a warrant!" Miss Lessing snapped. "No, I'm sorry, I have nothing to hide. Look all you want, I give you my permission! You're hurting me deeply, Mr. MacKenzie."

"Am I hurting you, Miss Lessing?" Ndula said.

"You!" Her face twisted in disgust for a second, and then she smiled. "Why, of course, Mr. Ndula. You hurt me too."

"Look around, everyone," ordered Chief Reynolds.

The chief, Bob, Pete, and Ndula spread out through the small house. MacKenzie remained in the living room with Miss Lessing.

"You'll regret this, MacKenzie," she said. "I know

nothing about the kidnappers or those two boys."

"How do you know there are two boys?"

"You just told me there was another boy named Jupiter!"

"No, we never said Jupiter was a boy," MacKenzie replied. "If you really didn't know him, you might assume he was a man. That's twice you've slipped. You knew back in the trade mission that there were two boys before we ever mentioned Jupiter. Have you identified Ian Carew for those extremists?"

"I have nothing more to say to you!"

Bob and Ndula came out of an inner room, and Pete and Chief Reynolds returned from the other side of the house. Bob faced Anna Lessing.

"I think you have some explaining to do, Miss Lessing," the Investigator said.

"Do I have to be bothered by children?" Anna Lessing complained to MacKenzie.

"You know," Bob said, "our friend Jupiter always says you have to observe the small things. He says people's habits always give them away. You're a Nandan, right? I'll bet you like Nandan jewelry."

"What is this boy babbling about? I warn you, MacKenzie—!"

Bob raised his hand. He was holding a small ivory tusk set in gold and attached to an earring hook for pierced ears.

"I found this in your bedroom, Miss Lessing. It's a Nandan earring, isn't it? There was only one in your room. That's because you lost the mate to it. I know because we found the mate in that box canyon where the helicopter landed to pick up the kidnappers."

Anna Lessing turned pale as she stared at the tiny tusk.

"Jupiter says that a woman almost never throws away an earring she likes when she loses its mate," Bob said. "You have that habit, and it proves you're one of the enemies of Sir Roger Carew. Besides the police and us, there were only three people in that canyon—the two kidnappers and the helicopter pilot. You were the pilot of that helicopter!"

19

The Last Laugh to the Enemy?

"Wow," Pete realized, "it could have been her under those goggles and the flying suit!"

"I expect we can find out if she's a pilot," Chief Reynolds said.

"The helicopter people should recognize her voice," MacKenzie added.

"And we have the matching tusk," Ndula finished.

Anna Lessing glared at them all. Hate and anger spread across her face. Then she laughed.

"All right, yes! I flew the helicopter, and I'm one of them! I always have been. I am a patriot of a safe, free, civilized Nanda!"

"Free for whom, Miss Lessing?" Ndula said quietly.

"Not for you!" the woman said fiercely. "Nanda belongs to the white people who settled it, built it, and have lived in it for two hundred years!"

"We have lived in it for two thousand years," the black Nandan said. "You built it on our work, by making us slaves in our own land. We will give you a place in our country, and work together for a free Nanda, but it is our country."

"Never!" Anna Lessing snarled. "We have made Nanda ours, we own it, we will keep it!"

Chief Reynolds said, "Your politics are your business, and you can settle your dispute in Nanda. But this isn't Nanda, and you have kidnapped two boys. The kidnappers were here, weren't they? Where are they now? Where are Ian and Jupiter?"

"Yes, Walt and Fred were here." Anna Lessing laughed. "But they're gone! You're too late!"

"Where have they gone?" MacKenzie demanded.

"You'll never learn that from me. Ian is in our hands, and Sir Roger will have to do what we want."

"No, Miss Lessing, he won't do what you want," MacKenzie said. "No matter what you threaten, he will do his duty for the future of Nanda. What you want would lead to a bloody civil war, and Sir Roger will never allow that to happen."

"You think he will risk his only son's life for the sake of a mob of uncivilized blacks?"

"Yes," Ndula said. "He will."

"Never! He will be forced to come to his senses and see that he is a white man and one of us!"

Chief Reynolds said, "I don't know what's going to happen in Nanda, but I do know that you're not going to be there to see it unless you cooperate now. Kidnapping is a very serious charge. Things will go easier for you if you help us to rescue those boys."

"I am a soldier in a war, not a kidnapper. This is a political action, and there is no way you will catch Fred and Walt now! No way you can rescue Ian Carew or that young fool Jones!"

She laughed in their faces. The two Nandans, Chief Reynolds, and Pete looked at each other in dismay. How would they ever stop the kidnappers and find Ian and

Jupiter if she would not talk? Only Bob did not seem disturbed. He was studying Anna Lessing thoughtfully.

"If the kidnappers weren't here when Miss Lessing drove home," Bob said slowly, "she must have told them how to identify Ian over the telephone!"

"Naturally I told them." Anna Lessing laughed. "A simple matter of a small scar. Ian had his appendix removed some years ago."

"In that case," Bob continued, addressing the men, "why did she rush home here? I mean, she'd given the kidnappers the information they needed, they knew which boy was Ian, and they must be putting their escape plan into effect now. So why did Miss Lessing leave work early and come to this house?"

"Bob's right!" Chief Reynolds exclaimed. "There was no need for her to come home at all."

"It's my home," Anna Lessing snapped. "Why shouldn't I come home?"

"Yes, but why in such a hurry?" Bob said. "The only answer I can deduce is that the kidnappers left something here that had to be watched! Something like Jupiter!"

"Jupiter?" Chief Reynolds frowned.

"Yes!" Ndula exclaimed. "They wouldn't take Jupiter with them if they are on their way to Nanda. Not once they knew which boy was really Ian! Taking two boys would be an unnecessary risk."

"Jupiter must be around here somewhere!" Pete cried.

"Search the place again!" Chief Reynolds ordered.

While Ndula remained with Anna Lessing, the others spread through the small house searching in every room and closet. It didn't take long. They found no sign of Jupiter.

"Try outside," MacKenzie urged. "The garage, any sheds."

Anna Lessing stood smiling as the searchers went outside. There was one small shed and a garage. They found only garden tools in the shed, and nothing at all in the garage. Pete scrambled all over the hillside above the house, but he found no trace of Jupiter.

Back in the small house, Anna Lessing taunted them.

"I told you you'd never find them. Admit it, MacKenzie, we've beaten you! And we'll beat you and Sir Roger and all the other weaklings in Nanda!"

"Search once more!" Chief Reynolds commanded.

It was growing dark inside the small house. The lush vegetation surrounding it was blocking the rays of the late afternoon sun. The searchers turned on lights to look under the beds and in the dark closets.

"Chief!" Pete cried.

Almost as soon as the lights went on, they began to flicker!

"What is it?" Ndula wondered. "A power interruption?"

The lights flickered again—on, off, on, off.

"No, the weather is perfect," Bob said slowly. "No storms. And it's not that hot, so I don't think there's any overload on the circuits."

More flickers, short and regular.

"It's almost as if someone's doing it," MacKenzie said. "Someone fiddling with a master switch, or a fuse, or—"

"Jupiter!" Pete cried. "I'll bet Jupe is trying to signal us. He *is* here somewhere!"

"But where? We've looked everywhere!" the chief said.

"Look, she knows!" Bob pointed.

Anna Lessing was no longer smiling at them.

"Chief," Pete said, "this house is built on a steep slope! The rear touches the ground, but the front is raised on pillars. There's a space under the house. Maybe there's a hidden cellar!"

Pete ran outside, and came back in a few moments.

"The house is built up on a concrete foundation like a big box," he reported, "but there's no door into the cellar from outside."

"Then there must be one inside," Bob declared.

"Pull back all the rugs," the chief ordered. "Look under the beds again. Try inside the closets."

Bob found the answer in the largest of the bedroom closets. There was a trap door in the floor with a narrow ladder going down into darkness.

"There's a light switch on the closet wall," Pete said.

Bob thumbed the switch, and a flickering light came on in the cellar area below. The two boys tumbled down the steep ladder into a small, windowless room. There were bottles of wine, stored furniture, and . . .

"Jupe!" Bob cried.

"First!" Pete yelled.

The overweight leader of The Three Investigators was sitting against the wall of the tiny cellar room, his hands tied behind him and a gag in his mouth, slowly kicking at the master switch on an old-fashioned fuse box! Each time he kicked the switch lever, the lights flickered!

"We knew the lights were a signal from you!" Pete crowed.

Bob quickly removed the gag and untied Jupiter's hands.

"Well, it's about time," the First Investigator said grumpily. "I could hear you all up there for the last hour. I thought you'd never figure out where I was."

"Gee, Jupe," Pete began, crestfallen. "We thought—"

"If you think you could have done better," Bob said hotly, "you can—"

Jupiter grinned. "Great work, fellows! Tell me how you got here!"

Pete and Bob hurriedly explained the series of deductions that had led them to Anna Lessing's house.

"Great detective work, fellows." Jupiter beamed. "I couldn't have done better myself!"

Pleased with the praise of their leader, Bob and Pete helped Jupiter up the steep ladder and out into the living room, where the chief, MacKenzie, and Ndula pounded him happily on the back.

"We're certainly glad to see you, Jupiter!" MacKenzie said.

"You should be proud of Bob and Pete," Chief Reynolds added.

"I am," Jupiter declared, and suddenly looked all around. "But where's Ian? Did the kidnappers get away?"

Ndula nodded. "I'm afraid so."

"You found your young fool," Anna Lessing said with a nasty laugh, "but you've wasted so much time you won't catch Walt and Fred now! We've got Ian Carew, and you'll never find him!"

Only Jupiter seemed undismayed by Anna Lessing's triumphant words. The stout First Investigator smiled.

"Well, now," he said, "I wouldn't be too sure of that."

20

Escape Plan!

Chief Reynolds called the Los Angeles Police, and they arrested Anna Lessing as an accessory to kidnapping. Then, acting on information supplied by Jupiter, they radioed the San Diego police, and the Nandans' Cadillac drove rapidly south toward the Mexican border.

"Very well, young man," Chief Reynolds said as Ndula drove the big car, "how are we going to stop the kidnappers from escaping with Ian?"

"Well, I'm not sure we can," Jupiter admitted, "but I believe we have a good chance. After the kidnappers identified Ian by his scar, they took him upstairs in that house, and I heard them talking on the telephone."

"To who, Jupe?" Pete demanded.

"To their confederates, I presume—in Tijuana, Mexico," Jupiter explained. "They announced that they had Ian for sure this time, and that the escape would proceed exactly according to plan."

"What plan?" Chief Reynolds asked.

"I don't know," Jupiter said. "They didn't say anything about what the plan was."

"Then how can we hope to—?" MacKenzie began.

"But I do know three vital facts," Jupiter continued. "The kidnappers are meeting someone on the Tijuana side of the Mexican border at precisely ten o'clock to-night for the next step in their escape plan. And they will cross the border right at Tijuana."

"But when, Jupiter?" Chief Reynolds asked. "They could cross at any time and wait in Mexico for their meeting."

"That's the third vital fact I heard. They said that they had something to do in San Diego, and would stop there until just before it was time to meet across the border. So they will be crossing shortly before ten o'clock tonight!"

"And we'll be there waiting for them!" MacKenzie cried. "Fine work, Jupiter!"

"We don't have to know their plan, or who they're meeting in Mexico," Chief Reynolds said, "because we'll stop them on our side of the border."

"Exactly, sir," Jupiter declared.

"Jupe?" Bob said slowly. "Will they be likely to cross the border with Ian in their car? I mean, wouldn't it be risky to try to cross openly? Won't they be in disguise, or maybe hidden in something?"

"Jupe, he's right!" Pete groaned. "They have to guess the police are after them by now, and the border is being watched. I mean, they'd know that MacKenzie and Ndula would notify the police, whether or not we boys were found."

"But," MacKenzie said uneasily, "if they're disguised or hidden, how will we spot them?"

"That's our job," Chief Reynolds said. "We're trained to penetrate disguises and spot hiding places. Anyway, we can cross that bridge when we come to it."

Jupiter only nodded thoughtfully as the big car raced

on south. It was dark when they arrived in San Diego just after nine o'clock. They met two patrol cars of the San Diego Police Department and drove straight on to the main border crossing.

"We have just about half an hour," Jupiter observed as he looked at his watch. "After that we can expect the kidnappers to attempt to cross the border at any moment."

"Them," Pete said in dismay, "and a thousand others!"

Long streams of cars and trucks and buses were passing along the multiple lanes of the border crossing! Every lane was packed bumper to bumper as the vehicles inched through the checkpoints and on into Mexico.

"How do you plan to identify them in all this, Chief?" MacKenzie wondered.

"The San Diego police have given their descriptions to all the border guards," Chief Reynolds explained, "plus a description of their Lincoln, and a description of Ian. The Mexican police have the descriptions also, and know about the meeting across the border. They'll be on the alert for anyone acting suspicious over there, although I admit their chances are slim."

"Why, Chief?" Bob asked.

"Because people are inspected more closely coming back into the States than going into Mexico, so there is more delay and greater chaos over there."

"And what do we do, Chief?" Ndula asked.

"We watch and wait."

They parked at the side of the road where they could see all the lanes. One San Diego police car parked near the center border booth, and the other parked on the far side of the road.

Then it was ten minutes to ten o'clock!

"Look!" MacKenzie pointed. "There's a blue Lincoln!"

They all sat on the edge of their seats as the big blue car inched up to the border checkpoint. The guard peered inside carefully as a San Diego policeman stood alertly behind him. Then the guard stood up and waved the big car on through!

"It wasn't them," Pete groaned.

"Unless they were too well disguised," Ndula said.

"I don't think any disguise will work," Chief Reynolds said. "The guards will carefully search any car with a boy of Ian's general age in it. Disguises can't help much when the police are looking for a certain number of people together."

"But wouldn't the kidnappers expect that?" asked Bob. "I mean, that any group of two men, one tall and one stocky, with a fat . . . er, I mean, stout boy, would be inspected extra carefully?"

Jupiter nodded. "I think so, Records. So I think they will attempt to cross in hiding. In some vehicle that crosses regularly, and that will excite little suspicion."

"Like those?" MacKenzie exclaimed.

Two buses approached the border. The San Diego police stopped them and boarded both. The watchers in the Cadillac could see the police moving slowly down the aisles of the buses. Then they saw the police get off, and wave the two buses on into Mexico.

"There isn't much chance, I'm afraid," Ndula said.

"I . . . I hope there is," Jupiter said uneasily as he stared at the long lines of vehicles passing across the border.

It was two minutes to ten o'clock!

"I think they've slipped through," Chief Reynolds said, shaking his head. "We had better contact the Mexican police and see if they can't spot the meeting over there. They—"

A loud beeping filled the Cadillac! Everyone jumped, and looked at Pete. The loud beeping was coming from his shirt pocket!

"My emergency signal!" Pete cried.

"Turn it off, Pete," the chief said. "We must—"

"No!" Jupiter grinned. "Take it out, Pete. See where it points! Everyone look at the vehicles and see if any of them look suspicious! The kidnappers are close by!"

Pete studied his signal. The arrow on the directional dial was pointing directly toward the lines of traffic. Everyone stared at the slow-moving vehicles. There were no blue Lincolns, and no buses now—just lots of cars and four or five trucks and vans.

"Come on!" Jupiter urged.

They piled out of the Cadillac and threaded their way among the slow-moving vehicles. In the middle lane was a battered truck with Mexican license plates and a sign painted on each side in Spanish announcing that it belonged to a Mexican lettuce farm. As it moved closer to the border booth, the arrow on Pete's directional signal pointed straight at the truck!

"That's it!" Jupiter cried. "Hurry!"

With the chief leading, they reached the closed truck just as it stopped at the booth. The guard was already raising the canvas covering at the rear of the truck. He looked inside, shook his head, and motioned to the San Diego police to pass the truck through.

"No!" Jupiter cried. "They're on that truck!"

The guard shook his head. "Sorry, son, there's no one in the cab except the Mexican driver, and the back's empty."

"It can't be," Jupiter protested. "Listen, our signal is beeping louder than ever!"

The strong beeping filled the night above the noise of the traffic. Chief Reynolds and Ndula raised the canvas cover at the rear of the truck again. The inside was totally empty!

"The signal must be malfunctioning," MacKenzie said.

Jupiter eyed the empty interior of the truck. Then he stepped to the side and studied the outside of the vehicle. His eyes glowed.

"No, Mac, the signal's working fine! Look, the outside of the truck is at least four feet longer than the inside. That front wall inside is a false wall!"

Two San Diego policemen and Chief Reynolds jumped up into the truck. The chief inspected the front wall and shook his head.

"There's no door, Jupiter."

"No. The kidnappers are clever. They must have had the wall built *after* they were inside! That's what they stopped for in San Diego! Tear down that wall!"

"Careful, Chief," Ndula warned, "they're armed!"

Chief Reynolds motioned the San Diego policemen to flatten themselves against the side walls of the truck. He drew his own gun.

"All right, we know you're in there! You're covered from all sides. Kick down that wall and come out with your hands up!"

There was a silence broken only by the endless noise of passing traffic and the loud beeping of Pete's signal.

Then the sound of breaking wood filled the truck. The wall split open, and Walt and Fred stepped meekly out with their hands over their heads! Walt saw Jupiter.

"You! How did they find you so soon? How the devil did you spot this truck?"

"Quiet!" Chief Reynolds snapped, and took their guns.

The San Diego policemen found Ian bound and gagged inside the false compartment, and freed him. He stepped out, smiling.

"Chaps! Am I glad to see you! How did you ever do it?"

"How, Jupiter?" Ndula demanded. "The signal did it, yes, but how did you get your signal into this truck? You couldn't have seen this truck before!"

"I didn't get the signal on the truck," Jupiter said, grinning. "*They* got it on the truck!"

"Them?" Bob and Pete exclaimed in unison.

"Remember back in our workshop when I told Fred about the bug in Ian's shirt pocket?" Jupiter said. "Well, I did that because I had my signal in my pants pocket, and I wanted to make him search Ian first. When he turned away from Ian I was so close behind Fred that he had to bump into me—and I slipped my signal into his coat pocket while holding onto him for balance!"

The stout boy beamed at everyone. "Fred had the signal in *his* pocket all the time. That's why he and Walt never spotted me using it. Its beeper was still turned off, so they couldn't hear it. And no one could see the flashing light—if it ever went on—because Fred's coat is thick and he was in the front seat alone!"

Walt glared at Fred. "You idiot!"

Fred glared back. "You fool! It was all your stupid idea!"

"Take them away," Chief Reynolds said in disgust.

Still raging at each other, the two kidnappers were led away. Chief Reynolds turned to Jupiter severely.

"You should have told us about the signal, Jupiter."

"I wasn't sure it would work, sir, and I didn't want you to count on it and fail to use all other means to spot them," Jupe explained. "The kidnappers could have found it, or changed clothes, or something. But I guess they were just too busy, and it worked!"

The chief smiled. "Yes, it did. Very good work, boys!"

The Investigators beamed. Ian smiled along with them, safe now, and no longer the frightened fugitive.

"Now my father can go ahead with his work," Ian said.

Side by side, he and Jupiter grinned, looking like a pair of overweight twins.

21

Hector Sebastian Offers Some Help

Several days later The Three Investigators visited Hector Sebastian at his home in the Santa Monica mountains. The famous author listened intently while the boys reported the entire story of Ian Carew's rescue.

"Great job!" the writer exclaimed when they finished. "All of you did really professional work on this case."

"Thank you, sir," Jupiter said somewhat smugly.

"Yes," Mr. Sebastian mused with a twinkle in his eye, "this time Pete and Bob showed they too are topnotch observers and deducers. In fact, you might say that they were the ones who really solved the case."

Pete and Bob grinned, and as Jupiter began to turn faintly purple, Pete quickly held out the tiny ivory-and-gold tusk that had betrayed Anna Lessing.

"Er, we thought you might like to have this as a memento of the case," Pete put in.

The writer took the earring ceremoniously.

"I'll treasure it, along with all the other prizes from your cases. But what about the crooks? What's going to happen to them?"

"Well," Jupiter said, still a bit annoyed, "the police could send them to prison for a very long time for such a serious offense as kidnapping."

"Which is just what they deserve," observed Mr. Sebastian.

"That's true," Jupiter agreed, "but this kidnapping was basically a political one involving citizens of another country. So the police have decided to deport the kidnappers back to Nanda instead of sending them to jail here. The Nandan government will punish them as it sees fit."

"Elections were held in Nanda yesterday," Bob added, "and the extremists were so discredited by the kidnapping that Sir Roger won easily. That means a big boost for Sir Roger's plan to achieve independence under the majority rule of the blacks."

"Sir Roger says he will let the kidnappers out in a few years," Pete said, "if they behave well and try to work with the majority."

"A good idea." Mr. Sebastian nodded. "Their crime was really due to overenthusiasm for their cause. They thought they were right—and that that justified anything. So, does that wrap up the case?"

"Well," Pete answered, "we've got one problem. We haven't thought of a good title for our write-up. Can you help us out?"

"Hmmm," the screenwriter said. "How about The Mystery of the Deadly Double?"

"That's perfect," said Bob. "Ian was Jupe's double and he almost was deadly to him!"

"It's a good name for another reason," Pete added, smirking.

"What do you mean?" Bob asked.

"Jupe is a little on the heavy side," Pete answered, "in case you hadn't noticed. So you could say he—or Ian, who looks just like him—is double the size of an ordinary person."

Everyone laughed except Jupiter.

"I fail to see the humor of that remark," the stout leader said stiffly.

"I'm sorry, First," Pete apologized. "I couldn't resist."

Jupe grinned at last. The boys thanked the writer and filed out. Left alone, Mr. Sebastian thought over the dangers and complexities of the case. No matter what his girth, Jupiter and his able deputies were trouble for any criminals they tackled. What mystery would The Three Investigators take on next?

THE THREE INVESTIGATORS MYSTERY SERIES

NOVELS

The Secret of Terror Castle
The Mystery of the Stuttering Parrot
The Mystery of the Whispering Mummy
The Mystery of the Green Ghost
The Mystery of the Vanishing Treasure
The Secret of Skeleton Island
The Mystery of the Fiery Eye
The Mystery of the Silver Spider
The Mystery of the Screaming Clock
The Mystery of the Moaning Cave
The Mystery of the Talking Skull
The Mystery of the Laughing Shadow
The Secret of the Crooked Cat
The Mystery of the Coughing Dragon
The Mystery of the Flaming Footprints
The Mystery of the Nervous Lion
The Mystery of the Singing Serpent
The Mystery of the Shrinking House
The Secret of Phantom Lake
The Mystery of Monster Mountain
The Secret of the Haunted Mirror
The Mystery of the Dead Man's Riddle
The Mystery of the Invisible Dog
The Mystery of Death Trap Mine
The Mystery of the Dancing Devil
The Mystery of the Headless Horse
The Mystery of the Magic Circle
The Mystery of the Deadly Double
The Mystery of the Sinister Scarecrow
The Secret of Shark Reef
The Mystery of the Scar-Faced Beggar
The Mystery of the Blazing Cliffs

(*Continued on next page*)

The Mystery of the Purple Pirate
The Mystery of the Wandering Cave Man
The Mystery of the Kidnapped Whale
The Mystery of the Missing Mermaid
The Mystery of the Two-Toed Pigeon
The Mystery of the Smashing Glass
The Mystery of the Trail of Terror
The Mystery of the Rogues' Reunion
The Mystery of the Creep-Show Crooks

FIND YOUR FATE™ MYSTERIES

The Case of the Weeping Coffin
The Case of the Dancing Dinosaur

PUZZLE BOOKS

The Three Investigators' Book of Mystery Puzzles